BY GRACE,
BY MERCY

B. AKISANYA

TABLE OF CONTENTS

CHAPTER ONE

The Lagos-Ibadan Expressway is an immersive portrait of hustling in Nigeria. The 127-kilometer stretch of road is its own ecosystem, filled with all kinds of life. It is Nigeria's first and main inter-state highway. Truckers freight goods, buses transport passengers, and regular commuters go about their personal businesses. Hawkers are like curtains for the Expressway, weaving in and out of slow-moving traffic. They offer commuters stuck in the ever-present gridlock an oasis with sachets of chilled pure water, *zobo, pito,* biscuits, and a smorgasbord of other quick snacks that can be quickly bartered for money. If the commuter is brave, they can buy *gala.* If Lagos had a state snack, it would be *gala.* Gala is a pastry rollup of buttery dough, casing well-seasoned sausage meat...but *gala* is not always what it is supposed to be.

The real champions of the Expressway are the pedestrians, the ones who brave crossing it at various points. Even with the recent upgrades to the Expressway, there is still no accommodation made for pedestrians, not an overhead walkway bridge or a crosswalk. Dogs – *really* fast dogs – have been steamrolled, trying to make it across the Expressway. And the driver simply drove on.

Lisa didn't enjoy the greenery punctuating the usual bustle of the Expressway too much as she drove back from Alaro village, though greenery is always a welcome respite for a city girl like Lisa more used to the concrete jungles of Ibadan and Lagos metropolis. She knew to always keep external and internal eyes on the road.

Lisa had departed Bethel Everlasting Stone Evangelical Ministries – BESEM – right after service was over, altogether skipping the after-service schmoozing. Soon after sending a text to Ken expressing her desire to purchase the Adagio lot, she'd received another one from Mama Abiye. Of course, the text came from Mama Abiye's son; the old woman did not do much texting or writing. The text had said Lisa's medical expertise was needed in Alaro village right away. Lisa periodically got similar texts, requiring her to load up her sedan with medical supplies and head to Alaro right away. The old woman never directed her son to message Lisa unless there was a maternal issue she couldn't solve, and those were few and far in-between. Lisa had once seen Mama Abiye stop preterm labor with herbs. This time, Lisa was needed for a labor that had failed to progress despite Mama Abiye's administration of fresh juices extracted from bitter leaf and the common yellow commelina or African yellow dayflower.

With empty crates moving around in the boot and backseat of Lisa's sedan, Lisa happily mulled all that she'd observed in Alaro. Once again, Lisa came away very impressed by Mama Abiye's care delivery to the local women and children, all with very limited resources. Lisa had been posted to Alaro Village for her National Youth Service Corps assignment - NYSC. Alaro was a small, remote village on the outskirts of the city of Lagos, about 45 kilometers out on the road towards Ibadan. The main dirt road leading to Alaro is accessible from the Expressway.

Calling Alaro village 'underserved' was a misnomer, as the village had no western medical facilities or personnel at all. Villagers received care for whatever ailed them from the village herbalist whose wife was also the doula of sorts for the pregnant women – Mama Abiye. Her husband was Baba Alagbo, named after his profession. Baba Alagbo prescribed herbs for ingestion at discretionary doses, topical application, vapor inhalation from boiling the herbs, or some other method of administration. With no specific formulary guiding the doses, some may find Baba Alagbo's sole discretion in determining appropriate dosage dangerous. Nevertheless, Baba Alagbo was quick to defend his methods by reciting his most prized metric: no one in his care has died because of his herbs. Of course, there was no way to vet this metric because most of the illnesses Baba Alagbo treated were not the kinds that killed anyway. No one that anyone knows has ever died from ringworm or piles.

Mama Abiye, on the other hand, provided maternal care to the village women for conditions that were much more serious than her husband's specialty; and she was very successful at it. She educated the young boys and girls on the virtues of abstinence and warned them of the responsibilities that resulted should they fail to listen. The village women trusted her implicitly; so much so, it had been difficult for Lisa and her NYSC group to make any impact at all. The villagers simply hadn't seen the need for their type of medicine. That Mama Abiye never demanded payment also made it easier for the village women to go to her. She never turned anyone away; she only took the goodwill offerings they gave her which ranged from nothing to small chickens.

In the end, Lisa and her NYSC group had surmised that the only impact they could make was with the small percentage of women that faced complications too difficult for Mama Abiye. For this population of women, Lisa and her team had supplemented Mama Abiye's care with western medicine. Beyond that, they'd left well alone. Though it has been years since Lisa finished NYSC, Lisa kept in contact with Mama Abiye. Unless Lisa received the call at night, she made it a point to get to Alaro within four hours of the initial call. Lisa was the village's dedicated emergency line.

Oddly, Mama Abiye's dedication to community maternal care had inspired Lisa to do the same for other low-income Lagosians. Also, an old friend from medical school who was well-travelled had once told Lisa that there were laws in places like America that prohibited a hospital receiving federal funds from turning away anyone in need of emergency care. Though there was no such law in Nigeria, Lisa hoped to seek funding from official and unofficial sources to enable the provision of care to low-income Lagosians regardless of their ability to pay. If Ken would sell her the vacant lot that used to house Adagio before it burned to the ground, and if he sold it at a reasonable price, Lisa planned to build a clinic.

Lisa dragged her happy musings from the inspiring Mama Abiye to how she would share her latest aspirations with her parents. Lisa knew her parents may not approve; she also knew that they could not stop her from doing it. The only person that could stop her was Ken, if he opted not to sell. Other than that, she was poised to buy, which is why she would test out the news on her roommate and best friend - Sylvia.

Though Lisa was resolved in her decision, she was hoping to finesse her parents' support. Afterall, if Lisa's plans are successful, her clinic and her parents' church would then become neighbors. And while Lisa was confident in the godliness of her intentions, she still didn't want to make bad neighbors with Pastor Dare. She hoped he would see this as a victory for a godly cause, instead of as an affront to his authority. Though Lisa was almost twenty-six years old, she still courted her parents' approval appropriately. She was Nigerian, after all. Lisa hoped to help her parents see that out of Adagio's ashes could rise something beautiful. Emeka – Lisa's brother – used to be the black sheep of the family, but he'd gone back to law school and was now on a good path. Unless Emeka joined a campus cult, which was unlikely, Lisa could very well be on her way to becoming the black sheep of the family.

***

"You did what?! You want to buy which building? Tell me, Lisa. Is it your parents you hate or Jesus? Because it must be one or the other."

"Let's not be too dramatic, Sylvia."

"*I* am being dramatic!? The building you want to buy was the subject of a whole drama series. Now you want to give it season two. And I'm the one that's dramatic?"

Lisa had informed her flat mate and best friend – Sylvia – about the text she'd sent to Ken about purchasing the now vacant lot that used to be Adagio. Lisa had been watching her phone ever since, waiting on a response from Ken. She'd watched her phone while she and Sylvia were making and eating their dinner. She'd watched her phone while they were cleaning the dishes and their kitchen.

"Sylvia, I really thought you of all people would support me. You know I've been trying to expand my

7

practice. This is a great opportunity to do that. Being closer to my parents is also a bonus. This has nothing to do with Ken."

"Except for the part where he owns the building. What about that part?" Sylvia continued to inject common sense into her best friend's decision-making. "This guy got into your head from day one. I have been telling you since, but you didn't listen. He cheated on you. You broke it off. Instead of you to let sleeping dogs be, you want to wake this dog of a man up."

"You're making it a bigger deal than it is. I can't imagine that Ken handles this kind of thing by himself. I may not even have to deal with him at all."

"Hmmm…. Do you even *want* to believe that?"

"It's the truth! You really think rich people go about selling their own properties by themselves? He'll probably just send me a contact to reach out to."

"And has he done that?"

That part. Ken has not responded.

"Not yet."

"Since morning that you texted him, he hasn't responded?"

"Nope."

8

"Hmmm…maybe this Ken guy has more sense than you after all. Maybe *he* sees no need to reprise the disaster."

"No, that's not it."

"So, please enlighten me why you think he hasn't responded."

"I don't know. But that's not it."

"Lisa," Syliva said, momentarily stopping all cleaning activities and focusing on the conversation, "you are my best friend, and I will support you no matter what. But I need to know what I am supporting. And that means you need to be honest with yourself about what you want with this guy. The text you sent him from church, I have to say I'm shocked because you don't do things like that. You need to be honest with yourself, *and* about what you want with this guy."

Lisa didn't have an immediate response to that. Or maybe she had a response, but she didn't want to admit it to herself yet.

"I'm just trying to buy a building. That's all."

Sylvia stared at her friend for a few seconds. "Okay," Sylvia acquiesced. "That's all it is then."

***

9

Later that night, Lisa looked over some patient files and finalized her notes for the patient records to be transcribed.

You need to be honest with yourself.

Her earlier conversation with Sylvia came back to her. Leave it to Sylvia to be the voice of her conscience, a redundant voice Lisa didn't need. She had her parents for that, especially her mom.

Lisa and Sylvia have been friends since their university days. Though Lisa had been in her third year by the time Sylvia gained admission to University of Ibadan, their sameness in age and involvement in campus fellowship had been commonalities they shared. The pair would eventually become roommates for the rest of Lisa's time on campus. Pastors Dare and Chi considered Sylvia their daughter, too. The two women's friendship had strained a bit while Lisa was in university at Ibadan only because Sylvia's education had been more normal paced than Lisa's. While Lisa had graduated from secondary school at 14 with honors, Sylvia didn't graduate until 17, by which time Lisa was already getting ready to graduate university. Now that Lisa was already a professional, Sylvia was finishing up a master's degree in University of Lagos while supporting herself with a side hustle. When Lisa moved back to Lagos, she'd been elated to reconnect with her best friend, and they have been flat mates ever since.

Lisa trusted Sylvia's counsel just as much as her parents, which is why she couldn't dismiss it if Sylvia was concerned. However, Lisa didn't see the need for the concern here. She was done with Ken in any romantic sense. She was certain of that, and she hoped Ken knew that as well. Nonetheless, being done romantically didn't mean she couldn't avail herself of this opportunity to expand her practice. Lisa hoped Ken saw it that way – a business transaction between two people. Nothing more, nothing less.

Just as Lisa was finishing up with patient notes and getting ready for bed, her phone chimed. Without needing to look, she knew it was Ken finally responding.

And she was right. The text from Ken said:

Of course. Meet me tomorrow and we can discuss.

Lisa continued to stare at her phone, half-expecting one of Ken's silly poems to chime through, some ill-rhymed attempt at a limerick about real estate. Nothing. Just primness and pleasantries. No *'hey, Lisa! So good to hear from you after such long while!"*

You need to be honest with yourself, Sylvia's words came back to haunt her again as Lisa got into her bed.

***

Earlier in the day...

Ken stood in front of what used to be Adagio and surveyed what was left of the location. He'd hired contractors to have the lot cleared, but before that, he'd hired a private engineering and fire damage assessor firm to work with the Lagos State Fire Service (LSFS) to assess the damage done to his building. He'd desperately hoped for a plausible explanation, perhaps a stupid patron had misplaced a lit cigar too close to a couch on the second floor. He'd even hoped for a vengeful explanation – an overzealous member of the neighboring church setting the fire. Nothing of the sort.

After weeks of investigation, his contractors and LSFS found that the fire did start on the second floor, somewhere behind the middle two pillars in front of Adagio. They said the height of the pillars, which was the tallest thing in the Lakowe area, may have attracted lightning strikes. And yes, they believed lightning struck those pillars multiple times. What no one could answer was how the fire spread so fast during heavy rainfall. And when he asked them to keep looking for answers, both his contractors and LSFS politely declined. Both establishments stopped short of saying what everyone else was thinking: the hand of almighty God was involved. Ironically, that had been the premise of Ken's lawsuit against the church that prayed for the fire to come down. Too bad it had been unprovable.

Ken ran his hands over the beard he'd recently decided to keep as he looked at the completely flat, empty lot, save the concrete-covered foundation. He took a furtive step towards where Adagio had stood. Though some might say he shouldn't have located a strip club next to a church, Ken had not actively sought to do so. He'd worked with a real estate firm to source the location and had not been directly involved until after Adagio was already being built. And though he'd seen the moral dilemma of the location, and he'd addressed it to his real estate contractor firm, Ken had not thought it a big deal otherwise. Afterall, the church and his strip club would operate during different hours of the day. Morality should never be legislated or imposed. Everyone should be free to do whatever they want to do. This is how Ken lived his life and what he expected from others. He'd not anticipated the fight that Pastor Dare had put up.

Ken had never believed God burned Adagio; not now, not when he'd sued the church had he believed it. The lawsuit had been a matter of principle. While Ken believed in the existence of God, he didn't think God paid that much attention or cared about human interactions. The lawsuit he'd forced his lawyers to initiate had been Ken taking on a man – Pastor Dare – who'd challenged him to a fight. Two men whose interests had collided; that was all. His last meeting with Pastor Dare was the last time he'd seen the pastor. That was now many months ago. Ken had avoided trips to the site of post-mortem Adagio; and the few times he'd been compelled to come here, Ken had timed his visit to ensure he didn't run into the Pastor.

Though his planned Abuja expansion fell through – relative to Lagos, Abuja was still very conservative – Ken had quickly pivoted to expanding to other areas of Lagos with several more *Suya* spots. The current crown of Ken's portfolio, however, was his new high-end restaurant. This restaurant was like the one in Victoria Garden City – VGC – he'd taken Lisa to on their first date in that it turned into a relaxed club at night. However, Ken's new restaurant/club – Black Diamond – catered to extremely high-profile clientele, and the night club portion required a membership that came with a hefty monthly subscription and was otherwise not open to the public…or strippers.

The rigor of starting Black Diamond had kept Ken's mind off Lisa. And in the months since the fire, he'd managed to restrain his thoughts of her to when his exhausted mind wandered helplessly in the half-wakeful minutes before he dozed off at night. In those moments, he allowed himself the luxury of wishing what could have been, what could still be. Those dreams had always been short-lived, until today when his phone chimed with Lisa's text. Suddenly, his far-fetched dreams didn't seem that unreachable anymore. Perhaps, Lisa, too, wondered.

Lisa's text prompted this trip to ground zero Adagio. She wants to buy his building. Ken had started and deleted responses to Lisa too many times to count. He hadn't been able to formulate the right response because he hadn't been able to discern Lisa's intention. He was sure of one thing: Lisa's interest wasn't limited to his building. *Come on!* Land was not that scarce in Lagos. Why his? The only answer he repeatedly came back to was that she wanted to maintain some connection to him, although his logical mind immediately rebutted that explanation. He didn't think anyone, let alone himself, was that lucky. Even if Lisa could overlook the ideological divide – which is how Ken saw Lisa's religious devotion – he didn't think Lisa could soon ignore the unspoken and unsettled differences between him and her father. And there was also the matter of Lisa walking in on him and Ije. Too much water had passed under the bridge, though he believed there was still hope.

Ken and Lisa had never spoken about Adagio since the day Lisa found out he owned the strip club located next to her dad's church. She hasn't been welcoming or open any discussion on the matter. Ken knew Lisa was stubborn and did not discuss matters that she'd already made up her mind about. But he, too, was stubborn, as she will soon find out. He, too, didn't give up easily. And he'd already made up his mind that Lisa was the one for him; so, if she wanted to dally around with his building, so be it. He would play along. Perhaps this building and land that had taken so much from him still held promises.

Ken took out his phone and fired off a text to Lisa, hoping his blasé tone would hide the effort he'd expended in achieving it. Lisa didn't need to know that he had no intentions of selling Adagio…at least not yet.

CHAPTER TWO

From where he sat at the head of the pulpit, Pastor Dare could see her make a surreptitious and hasty exit past the ushers and out the double doors of the church. She'd done the same thing the last four times she'd visited BESEM. She would arrive late – which Pastor Dare had initially pegged to simple tardiness – and she would leave during church announcements. By her third visit, Pastor Dare concluded this woman was deliberate in her arrival and exit. This was a woman who didn't want to be seen, yet she felt compelled to come to church with her two children in tow. He guessed their ages to be seven and five.

Pastor Dare alighted his pulpit and hurried after the lady, catching up with her just as she was about to exit the front gates of the church.

"Hello o! You're leaving us so soon," Pastor Dare said with a big grin to the surprised lady who looked like a deer caught in the headlight.

"I…I didn't want to cause any trouble sir. I was just leaving," she said.

"Oh no! No trouble at all! I just wanted to say hello before you left us today." Pastor Dare continued before also greeting her two children, "What is your name?"

"Filomena, sir."

"Ha, Sister Filomena! Very nice to meet you and your children. But now that I see you, your face looks familiar o. Have we met before?"

Pastor Dare could see his question troubled Filomena. She was hesitant to answer.

"Ehn…I…I used to work…dance at Adagio."

Understanding dawned on Pastor Dare, momentarily dimming his big smile. He must have seen her around at some point.

"Okay. Well, let me formally welcome you to BESEM. I want you to meet my wife when you visit us next Sunday. I will tell her I met you and that she should look out for you, if that's okay with you."

"That's fine, sir."

True to her word, Filomena came back the following Sunday and met Pastor Chi. In fact, she stayed till the end of service and met both Pastor Chi and Pastor

Dare. She told them about her husband who'd left for greener pastures in Canada when her younger child was only a year old. They'd emptied their bank accounts to fund his relocation with the shared understanding that when he settled in Canada, he would relocate Filomena and their two children, too.

The first thing Filomena had noticed was that her husband's calls had become fewer and farther in between. He was too busy and things weren't easy, he'd tell her. He'd ask her to be more understanding. Then the calls had stopped altogether only six months after he'd left. And only a year after his departure, Filomena found out that her husband had married another woman who was expecting their first child together. He'd blocked her on all social medial platforms and left her with nothing to raise *her* children with. Filomena had initially struggled for years to make ends meet and care for her children. It had been a hard struggle as those ends never actually met. Filomena had been too ashamed to seek help from her family who'd never wanted her to marry a Yoruba man. And when she'd swallowed her pride and sought help from them, they'd turned her away.

When Filomena's younger child fell and broke his leg, she'd had no money for the necessary medical treatment; so, Filomena had turned to her neighbor – a single woman who seemed to be living her best life – for a small loan. Her neighbor had instead *borrowed* her common sense and introduced her to the boss at Adagio. And that was how Filomena became a stripper at Adagio. The money had been unbelievably good, and the ends finally met.

"But when that fire happened, Pastor!" Filomena said to the Pastors, "Ha, it shook us o! We all knew it was God. It can only be God. *Fear hold me die! You mean God fit just show up? Fear catch me o!*" Filomena said to the raptly attentive pastors. "I didn't want my life to be like this," she continued. *"But as I no get choice, na condition make crayfish bend. But I'm not bending anymore! I want to go back to God. That is why I started coming to church again. I just can't find a job. The men want to sleep with me first before giving me a job and the women think I don't know have any qualification. And they are right! I stopped school after I got married and got pregnant. Pastor, I just want a job. I am not looking for free money. I want to work.

A found lost sheep needs real food, not just the bread of the Word, Pastor Dare thought to himself with a heavy sigh. Listening to Filomena's struggles saddened him. If only there was a way to help people like her get

20

back on their feet, teach them a vocation and set them up. Pastor Dare resolved that he would find a way for the church to help Filomena and her children.

"Sister Filomena, how can the church help you today?" Pastor Chi asked. "Do you have a place to stay?"

"I do for now. It's just that my landlord has increased rent again, and he also said I need to pay for another two years. And I don't have that kind of money anymore since I stopped working at Adagio. I don't even want to live in that house anymore! It is too expensive. I'm looking for another house, Pastor Chi."

"Okay. We will help you find a place and help with rent," Pastor Chi assured Filomena.

Though her husband had requested the meeting, Pastor Dare hardly said a word the entire meeting. Instead, he listened to Filomena's story and let Pastor Chi take the lead. Towards the end of the three's meeting, Pastor Chi also suggested that Filomena meet her daughter for a medical check-up, which was odd for Pastor Chi to volunteer her daughter's medical training as part of *her* ministry. Still, she thought Filomena was exactly the population that Adaolisa would want to help.

Later that night, after Pastor Dare and Pastor Chi had concluded their nightly prayers together, Pastor Dare decided to stay longer in their prayer room. His heart was heavy within him over the problems Sister Filomena was facing.

A found lost sheep needs real food, not just the bread of the Word, was the constant refrain of his racing mind. A baby Christian needs to be cared for or the world would snatch them back, he thought. Pastor Dare had always wanted his church to serve people like sister Filomena in the community, people who were making their way back to Jesus and wanted a little help with the troubles of life. God would help such; so, the church should do what God would do. Just thinking about it couldn't help sister Filomena. Pastor Dare asked God to show him how to help Sister Filomena and people in similar situations. He asked God to bless BESEM to be a greater blessing to the community they were located in.

***

Lisa's busy day started with the bad decision to skip breakfast. She planned a stop at her own clinic before heading to the obstetrics clinic at Lagos University Teaching Hospital – LUTH. She was meeting Ken later in the evening and had packed a change of clothes for the meeting. At her clinic, her first patient was a single mom of two children – Filomena – referred to Lisa by her parents.

"So, tell me, Ms. Filomena, what brings you in today? Any recent changes in your health?"

"Ehn…Dr. Lisa, I just want to do checkup…general checkup."

"Okay. Is there any particular reason why you would be concerned for your health?"

"Ehn…no o. Is just that my work, the work that I had before, was….ehn…I just want to do general checkup *sha*."

"Okay," Lisa hesitantly agreed. It didn't seem she would be getting more out of Filomena, although Lisa was curious about the type of work that necessitated a medical workup.

Lisa called for her nurse and fired off instructions on the blood draw and the lab tests they would run. Though the clinic was supported by two nurses, one of the nurses had called Lisa to say she had car trouble and couldn't come into the clinic until much later.

"Ehn…I know you," Filomena stated with a gentle smile on her face. "I know you don't know me, but I know you. We all knew you."

"I'm sorry. Have you been here before?" Lisa asked as she paused in the middle of registering Filomena's blood pressure.

"Ehn...we didn't meet but that time you came to Adagio, we all saw you."

Lisa absorbed the information before asking, "You worked at Adagio? What did you do there?"

"Ehn...I was one of the dancers," Filomena responded with the same shy smile. Filomena was a conundrum to Lisa. She just seemed too innocent to live in Lagos. And now, Lisa finds out she also used to dance at Adagio.

"Is this why you are concerned for your health? Were you exposed to something at Adagio? I heard some of the girls took...personal clients...sometimes..."

"Me I didn't do that o! Because Boss Ken didn't like that. And I didn't want to risk it. Other girls did it *sha*."

"Okay. Well, your blood pressure and sugar look good. My nurse will come and take a blood draw, but we won't get the results for some of the tests today. Leave your phone number with them and we'll get the results to you. I also want to check your children, if that's okay?"

"They are fine. Don't worry, Dr. Lisa."

"Okay. But if they need medical treatment, just come in, okay."

"Thank you o, Dr. Lisa. Ehn…I have some money now but I can pay the rest-"

"Don't worry about it," Lisa interrupted. "It's already taken care of. Feel free to come in if you or your kids need any treatment."

"Dr. Lisa thank you o. My God will bless you. You are such a good person. That is why we were all so mad at Ije for what she did. Boss Ken really liked you and Ije just messed everything up. Since I started working at Adagio, I have never seen her give that man rest for one day. I don't even know why he didn't sack her."

"It's okay. It's all in the past now."

"Past? How? Dr. Lisa, don't tell me you won't forgive that man o. You have to o! Boss Ken really liked you. We all knew. Ije will no-"

Lisa interrupted Filomena's travel down memory lane. She really didn't want to hear it at all. Whatever went on between Ije and Ken at Adagio was their own business. And she was certainly not going to discuss it with her own patient.

Filomena's shy smile was back. "Thank you for your help, Dr. Lisa. You and boss Ken fit together. You help people. Don't worry; God will punish Ije."

A chuckling Lisa helped Filomena off the cot and onto her feet. Filomena reunited with her children who had been playing in the makeshift nursery beside the nursing station as they all headed out of the clinic.

Lisa was amused that Filomena would equate her work with what Ken was doing: they were both helping people, she'd said. Ken thought the same thing about his work, although Lisa didn't see it that way. Lisa believed like her father: there were better ways to gainfully employ someone off the streets than have them take their clothes off and dance for money. Of that, Lisa couldn't be convinced otherwise. Ken was the man at the helm. Adagio was Ken's business, which he located beside a church, no less. Ken employed strippers to dance at Adagio. Ken knew dancers were taking on private clients and didn't put a stop to it. Ken refused to move his debauched business elsewhere. Ken. Ken. Ken. It was him at the center of it all, not Ije.

After finishing her shift at the obstetrics clinic at LUTH, Lisa hurried through traffic to Ken's office. Lisa smoothed her hands over her hair for the umpteenth time. She dashed a glance at her reflection in the makeshift mirror that was the stainless-steel-finish walls of the elevator as she rode up to Ken's office. She'd drifted in and out of sleep all last night, telling herself her nervousness was really excitement, excitement at the prospect of purchasing and building *something* she could call her own. That Ken currently owned the building couldn't be the reason for her excitement, Lisa told herself. Her choice to wear a rather fitted shift dress and stilettos instead of her customary jeans and converse was really because this was a business meeting and she wanted to look the part, Lisa told her herself. And as she was directed into Ken's office by his assistant, her palms did a last run over her pulled back hair.

Lisa found Ken standing by a large window that overlooked the business district, though he was looking directly at the door. He had one hand in his pocket and the other hanging loosely by his side. He was dressed in his usual suit and simple white shirt, unbuttoned at the top, no necktie. Lisa noticed Ken was now spotting a full beard, which gave him a darker look.

They exchanged pleasantries. Lisa ignored Ken's open perusal and appreciation of her look.

Lisa said, "I want to be very clear that this is only about the building. Nothing else."

"Okay." Ken agreed with amusement and barely hidden mischief written all over his face. "Will you at least have a seat?"

"I am serious, Ken."

"I heard you. You've made it very clear that we're done. I don't like it, but I hear it."

"There is no future for us after what happened."

"Something I'll probably regret for the rest of my life. I still think there can be a future. But that's not why you're here and I don't want to hijack your meeting," Ken continued as he took charge of the meeting. "So, you want to buy my building."

"Yes, at fair market value."

Amateur, Ken thought, smiling to himself. *In this Najia? The market value is what I say it is.*

Out loud, Ken said, "Good. I'm glad you're not looking for handouts." He named an exorbitant price for the building, way above the market value.

"*Haba,* Ken! Come on!" Lisa exclaimed. "You and I both know that building is not worth that much. Let's not forget it's not *actually* a building. It's an empty lot."

"With a foundation laid for a two-story building." Ken paused before continuing, "You're also forgetting one other thing."

"Which is what?"

"I am not motivated to sell," Ken responded. "I took this meeting only because of *you*…I wanted to see you."

"Ken, all we can be now is just friends –" Lisa began but Ken cut her off.

"I know what you said. I respect it. I just wanted to see you. The truth is I don't have any plans to sell." Ken paused to let his words sink in for Lisa. "In fact, I have begun buying up more land around Adagio. I don't know what I want to do yet, but I'm not leaving that area."

"Are you serious right now?"

"Yes. Lisa, your father will need to get used to having me around," Ken shrugged. "I'm not going anywhere. He's going to have to get along with me."

"How is that going to happen? I feel like you're challenging him to another showdown."

"I'm not," Ken denied simply. "Just like the first time, I made several attempts to be neighborly with him and the church; *he* rebuffed me every time. He is the one with the problem, not me."

"You should know something about my father. He is not one of those hypocritical Christians. My father walks what he talks. I have never caught him in a lie."

"Oh, I know. Trust me, I do. I'm just not going to run, Lisa. That's not what I do."

Ken's revelation did not sit well with Lisa at all. "Do you have some morbid desire to challenge God or something?"

"Is that what I'm doing, challenging God?" Ken inquired through a chuckle.

"Yes! I'm pretty sure Pastor Dare is BFF with Jesus. Ken, you cannot build another strip club near Bethel Everlasting Stone Evangelical Ministries."

"Lisa, your father is not God. Frankly, I don't think God had anything to do with the burning of Adagio."

"But that's why you sued the church and my dad."

"Because I don't walk away from a fight. I don't start fights, but if you bring a fight to my doorstep, you best believe I'm going to finish it. Your father declined my hand of friendship and did whatever he did to burn my building. And you expect me to think *God* did it? And I should spare the man who, to me, is responsible for the damage? I won't do that. It's the principle, too, Lisa. No one gets to *take* things away from others just because you disagree with them; that's not how *we* live. Your father took my building... took my girl. I'm not packing up and running. We are going to remain neighbors until he learns to get along with me."

His girl. Lisa didn't acknowledge or respond to that reference. What shocked her was Ken's passionate defense of his position, which would be admirable, except that position was staunchly against Lisa's father. The truth is Lisa agreed with Ken: no one should use their beliefs to injure others. However, that rule, like every other rule, didn't govern God. God can do whatever He pleases. This much Lisa knows: if God had anything to do with the burning of Adagio, there was a larger purpose for it that would bring glory to His name.

"So, that's why you sued the church?"

"I don't run from a fight. Your father started it. And I wanted to finish it…and it's not over yet."

"Ken, you can try to make my father the face of your problems, but you and I both know that my father is not the reason why we are not together."

In Ken's mind, this was another opportunity to beg again. Ken sent a silent prayer up to the God of his mother for help. He took a moment to gather himself before speaking, his voice much more subdued.

"I know that. And I can't tell you how much I hate myself for what I did. It wasn't until I saw *that* look on

31

your face, and then you walked out and the reality of losing you settled in that I realized that there was no *pleasure* without you. Lisa...I have not been celibate since I was 16," Ken pleaded but he could see Lisa wasn't buying it. Still, he continued, "I wanted to...for you. There was so much going on...I was stressed...In my mind, we weren't exclusive yet, and...I thought I could get away with it. That is the truth. I am sorry."

Lisa shook her head back and forth, as though doing so would keep his words out of her ears. If Ken didn't want to sell the building to her or anyone, then there was no reason for her to be in his office. Lisa didn't want this to be about her.

Except there was no denying that it was entirely about her. It didn't take a genius to figure out that Ken was also holding on to what was left of Adagio because of the connection to her.

"Ken, we are done," Lisa repeated emphatically.

"I heard you."

"But you don't accept."

"No, I heard you; and I respect your decision. But *you* texted me. And I'm going to make use of every opportunity to convince you to give me another chance. This is just another one I lost. Another one will turn up."

He didn't say anything beyond that; he didn't need to. Mischief was written all over his face.

Some men moved over the threshold of good looking, past the precipice of handsome, straight on to beautiful. It occurred to Lisa in that moment, as she allowed herself the unfettered, unbridled luxury of taking in Ken's features, if only this one time, that this man was *fine*. His angular face and set jawline were deeply masculine and commanding, and the growing beard made those features downright dangerous, like he was Leonidas and his 300 all by himself. Yet, those same features softened with the flirtatious dimples indenting his cheeks. And the natural upturn of his right eyebrow was playful and wicked, like he baited you to dare him and find out. Ken's skin was darker than Lisa's; it was splayed rich mocha with freckled accents of dark chocolate. Lisa thought Ken's face was a work of art, masterfully crafted for a woman's viewing pleasure...beautiful.

You need to be honest with yourself. Sylvia's words came back to Lisa. At least Ken was clear on what *he* wanted. Ken had stayed away from contacting Lisa since that day outside the courthouse. He'd respected her request, and he'd stayed away...until Lisa texted him.

Lisa considered herself mentally strong. Equivocation was entirely out of character for her. One didn't navigate the halls of University of Ibadan as a teenage medical student without having some grit. And part of her mental strength was steadiness and a quickness at decision-making. Second-guessing oneself can prove fatal in Lisa's line of work. And that's exactly what Lisa was doing with Ken; she knew *that* for sure. She was second-guessing her principle that cheating was always a dealbreaker. She was second-guessing her decision to walk away from Ken and never look back. And she knew why,

The first time she'd seen Ken was in the hallways of Ward C of LUTH as he was escorted to one of the private rooms, and her first impression of him was that he was very tall. She'd also noticed the square of his shoulders and thickness of his neck. Lisa's mom had always gotten on her case for her bad posture, which she'd often overcorrected with a pronounced upright standing that was weird to the eyes of the onlooker and harder on her lower back. But Ken's posture was perfect; and he'd made it look so easy.

With Ken's sizeable donation to the hospital, the medical director had assigned the best available doctor to him, which was her.

She'd noticed the mischief in his eyes right away. Ken had shamelessly flirted with her and had wasted no time hitting on her. While that was not an unusual occurrence for Lisa, Ken's smoothness was confident. Like his cologne – which smelled like vetiver and sandalwood had a baby – Ken was unapologetically masculine in a way that invited you closer for a better whiff. And she was ashamed to say she'd done just that under the guise of listening to his lungs. And the word that scent had conjured was home.

All of Lisa's past relationships had grown out of friendships. Instant attraction had been unfamiliar to Lisa. Frankly, she'd expected the initial attraction to fizzle during their first date. He would, as they usually do, say something shockingly mid like, *'It doesn't matter all the degrees a woman has, she will still end up in a man's kitchen.'* Only Ken hadn't; on the contrary, Ken had been vocal about his admiration and respect for her profession. And her interest had grown with each conversation, each silly text, each phone call. She'd rationalized dating a nominal Christian. In many ways, Ken was a better person than some of the Christian brothers she'd met. Ken had respected her and treated her better than most Christian brothers. Ken had not been intimidated by her success and didn't require her to stop her work. Ken's commitment to family resonated with her. Ken had respected her choice to be abstinent...until he hadn't.

Sufficient emotional detachment is an important element of the medical profession, something Lisa had mastered. But seeing Ije bent over Ken's lap had sliced an unfamiliar pain through Lisa, one she'd not been able to face. And she'd declined any explanation from Ken and made it abundantly clear there was no hope for their relationship. Lisa had not even spoken to Sylvia about that day except to say Ken had cheated on her. And Lisa tells Sylvia everything, but she hadn't been able to vocalize this one, despite many attempts by her friend. Telling meant reliving it and Lisa didn't want to. It hurt too much because it was Ken. What had started as curiosity and morphed into attraction had developed into something deeper and difficult to walk away from. Sylvia was right after all: Lisa's intentions had very little to do with buying the Adagio building.

"It was a mistake coming here. I'm going to go."

"Don't go. I know I hurt you. Please...let's just talk. Ace, I messed up. I know I messed up. Please forgive me." Ken pleaded his case, following Lisa to where she'd gone to stand by the window.

"Ken, it's not about forgiveness. I forgive you, but it goes against everything I stand for to ignore what happened and plunge myself into a relationship with you. It would be...*stupid*. And I'm not stupid."

"I regret that day so much, Ace. I thought I could –"

"I don't want to talk about this, Ken!" Lisa interrupted Ken.

"Ok," Ken acquiesced out of respect. The last thing he wanted was to cause Lisa any more pain. "Ok. But I know my building is not the only reason why you contacted me. And I didn't take this meeting so I could sell a building. There are unresolved matters between us, Lisa."

The pair concluded the meeting, which Lisa thought was unsuccessful for many reasons, though Ken thought differently. He thought there was hope for something to bud yet again. And he promised himself to fan that flicker into a flame.

Shortly after Lisa's departure from Ken's office, a telling chime rang through on her phone. It was a text from Ken.

Why did the chicken cross the street?

...Because I love you.

Lisa didn't respond. Ken wasn't selling his building. There was nothing for Lisa to tell her parents after all.

CHAPTER THREE

"Pastor Chi, will you be able to preach on the third Sunday of next month?

"Okay," Pastor Chi responded absentmindedly.

Pastor Dare was setting up rosters for various church activities, and he had been rambling on about various topics for the last few minutes. It was clear to him that his wife was neither interested nor listening.

"I am also going to marry Elder Gbada's wife."

"Okay," Pastor Chi responded again before the import of her answer settled in. "Make sure to clear it with Elder Gbada first." Pastor Chi amended. "Sorry, I wasn't listening."

"That much is clear to me. You almost gave your darling husband away!" Despite his levity, Pastor Dare could see something was bothering his wife. "Is everything okay, Chiamaka? You've been unusually quiet all morning."

"I had a dream."

"Was it a troubling dream?"

"I don't know. I honestly don't know what to make of it," was Pastor Chi's pensive response. "I dreamt that we were walking to church as we usually do on Sunday mornings, me, you, Adaolisa and Emeka."

"Okay…what's troubling about that?"

Gazing squarely at her husband, Pastor Chi said, "There were three other people with us."

"Who? The Father, the Son, and the Holy Spirit?" Pastor Dare said with an ill-timed attempt at humor.

"Be serious, Dare."

"Okay, sorry. Who were the other three people?"

Without breaking gaze, Pastor Chi said, "A little boy and a little girl… and their father." Pastor Chi paused before she said, "And their father was Kene."

She watched as her husband took in the narrated dream, and also as he began to shake his head from side to side, all traces of humor gone from his countenance

"No way. No way in the name of Jesus Christ!"

"Dare, I think Adaolisa is going to mar - "

With speed like she'd never seen before, Pastor Dare flew across the table and placed his palm over his wife's mouth, stopping her from finishing the sentence she was about to make.

"Don't say it. Don't give it life, Chiamaka. It will not happen in Jesus Name!"

Pastor Chi saw her husband do something she'd never seen him do – panic. She saw trepidation in his eyes, clear as day.

"He is not good for her. He will not take my first fruit. I reject it in Jesus Name!"

"My husband, are you rejecting it because you know it is the will of God or because you don't like Kene? Remember, I am not his biggest fan either. But you and I know that our daughter has gone and fallen in love with this man."

"They are no longer dating. She assured me as much."

"She is still sniffing around him."

"Matters of the heart take time to resolve sometimes. That's all there is to it."

"I'm glad you know this is a matter of the heart. My question to you, my husband, is when have you known Adaolisa's heart to change its mind?"

Pastor Dare didn't have an answer to that question. Since birth, Adaolia had done things her own way, down to being born a full month after her estimated due date. Adaolisa was staunchly stubborn.

"Still, this man is not good for her."

"I know. You said I shouldn't say it or give it life and I have kept quiet o. But we need to pray about this."

"I agree with that. Lisa cannot …God forbid!" He couldn't bring himself to even say the word.

***

Ken stood in a darkly lit corner of the second floor of Black Diamond. This place was not like Adagio. Black Diamond was opulent and exclusive with just the right amount of traffic. It catered to some very powerful people who wanted to enjoy the nightlife away from prying eyes, *nouveau riche* whose name carried international influence and preferred to avoid reputational damage. They were tech giants, CEOs who employed software developers, fund managers and the likes. Black Diamond was an upscale restaurant by day and an exclusive club by night. Unlike how he'd managed Adagio – which was from his office, leaving Bosco and his boys to run things – Ken built a relationship with this crowd because it was good for business.

He spotted one of the clients he'd not seen in a while – Tade. Tade was a West African tech giant who'd married his dead brother's wife – Evelyn. Regardless of how it had started, Tade and Evelyn seemed to be going strong. They sometimes visited Black Diamond together, but not tonight. Tade was sitting by himself in one of the VIP corners, fending off persistent middle-aged women vying for his attention. Ken was on his way to Tade when Bosco approached him. What Bosco whispered was not what Ken wanted to hear, yet it filled him with excitement as he ran his hand over his beard. Ken took only moments to consider his actions before telling Bosco to lead him towards where Ken needed to handle business.

No matter how exclusive a club was, unsavory and unwelcome guests could still find their way in. Ken didn't care what his paying members did; but he could not have them being turned like tricks by *oloshos* and *runz girls*. Black Diamond was not a place where any grade of prostitute was allowed. It was easy for Bosco and his boys to spot the solo practicing *runz* girls but there was a particular group of women who showed up nightly, dressed to kill in top designers. To the average onlooker, these ladies were Lagos big girls, but trained eyes knew they were there to work. These ones didn't approach rich men and women. They played the game so well that the rich men and women approached them. They blended in well. They carried themselves very well. They were okay with not scoring a mark every night. But when they caught a prey, they latched on like a leech and bled them dry: drugging and blackmail was how they got their mark to part ways with millions of Naira. Chief Saka – a logistics magnate with a veritable shipping line – had been one of Black Diamond's first members until he'd fallen prey. He'd just stopped coming. And when Ken followed up with him, with some pressure, Chief Saka had revealed that he couldn't come to a place where prostitutes also came to. Ken had immediately tasked Bosco with finding who was responsible for Chief Saka's troubles.

Bosco had been trailing these women, and he'd found out that they got their invitation from one of the paying members, but the member himself or herself had never set foot on Black Diamond. Until tonight. Bosco had told Ken that they'd found who they believed to be the owner of the membership account and were holding him in one of Black Diamond's back rooms, which is where Ken was now headed.

The person Ken saw sitting in the chair in the middle of the otherwise empty room couldn't be called a man. He couldn't be a day over twenty. This guy couldn't be the one in charge of all those men and women.

"This is how you treat your members!? Do you know who I am!?" Little Pimp said, masking his fear with bravado. "I pay good money for my membership! What's all this embarrassment!? Your boys don't know what they are doing and you're going to lo-"

Ken stunned Little Pimp's left cheek with an open fist. It was suddenly important to Ken to let him know that the bravado was not working.

While Little Pimp was still wincing from the pain of the hit to the fast-swelling left side of his face, Ken said, "I'll say this once. Give me the name of your boss."

"I don't have a boss, you moth-"

Ken's closed fist connected with the left side of Little Pimps face again. Ken was unaware of the chagrined look on the faces of Bosco and his boys. To them, Ken was acting strange. Ken almost never entered these backrooms; such... enforcement actions were usually left to Bosco and his boys. But then, Ken hadn't been feeling like himself lately. And Little Pimp was going to bear the brunt of that.

"Give me the name of your boss," Ken repeated.

"I'll have you arrested! Do you know who I a-"

Ken's blow to Little Pimp's solar plexus knocked the air clean out of him. He bawled over in pain, but Ken didn't relent. The darkness that had loomed for months had finally touched ground over Ken. He delivered blow after blow until Bosco pulled him off Little Pimp.

"Boss, you're going to kill him!"

Ken could read the alarm on Bosco's face and it annoyed him. "Get your hands off me now," Ken said through gritted teeth.

"I can't let you do that. I'll take care of it."

Ken broke free from Bosco and was about to land another blow on Little Pimp who was now bloodied and curled up in a fetal position before his feeble voice said, "Ije…Ije."

Somehow, Ken wasn't surprised.

"I am going to give you a message to give to her," Ken said menacingly, intentionally sidestepping the name that he'd vowed would never pass through his lips again.

Ken's message to Ije was non-verbal but very clear on Little Pimp's face and whole body.

***

"Boss, mama called. She said she has been trying your number but no answer. She said you should call her back," Bosco said to Ken as he drove to Ken's house later that night.

It was unusual for Ken to avoid his mom's call. They talked almost every day but that had stopped recently. Ken had just not been in the mood for catch-up conversations. So, true to Nigerian mom form, his mom had called the person she knew was always with him. He knew his mom did not only have Bosco's phone number; she also had the phone number of every one of Bosco's boys and every employee that was manager or above in all of Ken's establishment. *They are part of our work family,* his mom would say. But Ken knew better; it was precisely so she could phone-stalk him if she couldn't reach him. Only she didn't have to use all those numbers. She only had to call Bosco and Bosco – who was otherwise loyal to him but would gladly lay down his life for Ken's mom – would hound him until Ken capitulated and called.

Ken's eyes met Bosco's judgy eyes in the rear-view mirror from the back seat of his Bentley where he'd been trying to stretch out the kink that taken residence in both of his shoulders.

"You have something you want to say to me, Bosco?"

"I just talk am now, Boss. Mama said you should call her back" Bosco said with uncharacteristic impatience.

Ken's eyes held Bosco's in the rear-view mirror. "Why don't you focus on your business and let me focus on mine." Ken wasn't referring only to his mom's call. He thought Bosco's interruption when he was dealing with Little Pimp earlier in the day was disrespectful.

There was silence in the car for a few minutes before Bosco responded. "I am not going to stand by while you beat someone to death. If you want to become the guy who kills people, let me know so I can look for another job. I have seen enough death in my life."

"You've not punched anyone before?"

"I have. But it's my job. And I know how to do it so nobody dies on my watch. You want to go Shina Rambo? Let me first leave. *When woman nyansh spoil finish everybody go leave im nyansh for am* "

Ken rolled his eyes at yet another one of Bosco's *nyansh* proverb but otherwise didn't respond. Bosco was right that Ken preferred not to sully his hands. But people keep thinking his niceness was a weakness and he was not having it anymore. It had felt good beating that lesson into Little Pimp. Ije would read it loud and clear.

Bosco continued, "I don't know what's going on with you o, Boss. But you have to do something about it."

47

The next day...

"American boy. How your fine body? Long time, no see. What is this I hear that you're getting soft? The last time I saw you, you were....hard. *Dat your girl still no dey gree you knack?"*

Fewer things were more pathetic than a retired *runz* girl. Though Ken would prefer that she wasn't siting across him, Ije had slithered into Black Diamond the following night and finagled her way up the stairs to sit at his corner. Ken observed Ije, whom he'd not seen face-to-face since the night Adagio burned to the ground. She'd aged ten years in ten months. Lines were starting to gather around her once-vibrant eyes, but it wasn't even that; it was the coldness in them that aged her the most, like hope had left the building. Last time he'd seen that look in Ije's eyes was when Ken had first met her.

While Ken had rehired everyone who worked with him in Adagio, he'd cut off all contact with Ije. He blocked her on all platforms and told her in no uncertain terms to never contact him again. Though Ken knew what Lisa had caught he and Ije doing had been entirely consensual, seeing Ije was too much of a reminder of all it had cost Ken. He much preferred the constant reminder in his own mind to the one in Ije's image. He guessed Ije didn't like being cast off and was now reaching out from the pit he'd buried her.

"American boy, why you do my guy like dat now? You show that guy shege o. Him still dey hospital. Why you take do am like dat now?"

"Was I not clear when I told you to stay away from me?"

"Abeg calm down," Ije continued "Nobody wants you o! Guy, I'm all about business."

"Good for you. But do your business elsewhere. Black Diamond is not the place for your…people."

"Is that judgment I detect? You think you're better than me now? As I recall it, you used to keep girls, too. I was one of them."

"That's not what you're doing. You are pimping men and women out."

"You pimp *prostitutes*. My girls and guys are anything but. They are high class escorts catering to very high-class clientele. And Black Diamond is now the place to meet high-class clientele."

"You forgot the drugging, compromising pictures and blackmail."

"Ehn ehn, is it your blackmail? Are they complaining?"

What Ken heard in Ije was not wickedness; it was more sinister than that – hopelessness. He knew that feeling well. This was the same Ije that had vowed to him that she would not return to the lifestyle she was now hosting for others to live in. But after he cut ties with Ije, Ije had blown through her savings and returned to the only thing she knew to do, only she'd scaled her operation by recruiting others to elongate her reach. He looked at her with pity because of what desperation had done to her. Yet, he also felt guilty because he thought he had a hand in Ije's downfall. He'd never intended to hurt Ije, yet he had, which is why he found himself saying, "If you need money…"

"I don't want your money. I don't *need* your money. I make mine now."

"By pimping? You were hurt by *that* and you're doing the same thing to others."

"My girls and guys are well taken care of."

Ken heard his own words in Ije weak defense. He'd been convinced that keeping women who took their clothes off to entertain others was just fine. He'd had no reason to examine or alter the way he made money until he'd seen *that* look in Lisa's eyes. And even now, he wasn't too far from where he was, but at least there were no strippers at Black Diamond.

"Good for you," Ken responded. Ije was on her own journey and was free to find out for herself. "But you cannot do it in my place. Make sure none of your people set foot in Black Diamond again. The last message I sent you will be tame compared to what will happen next time," Ken finished menacingly.

"B*ig blokus dey scare woman with pikin?* You don't scare me o, Ken. I know you. *You no fit do anything. You? Mtchew... you be good guy now.*"

Ken chuckled mirthlessly as he ran his hands through his full-grown beard and considered Ije's words.

"For both our sakes, I hope you're right," Ken said as he brushed his hands over his full-grown beard before he motioned for Bosco to come escort Ije out of his club.

CHAPTER FOUR

"Boss, *wetin dey sup? Dis your face is not looking normal at all o.*" In all of Bosco's years working with Ken, he'd never seen his boss like this. Bosco knew Ken better than most people. Bosco had been at the airport with a gang of criminals notorious for breaking into vehicles parked in the multi-level parking structure servicing Murtala Mohammed International Airport (MMIA). He'd not been activated to start participating in the criminal activities; he'd been there to observe before participating. And that's how he met Ken, who was still in college at the time and looked very different than now. For one thing, Ken had worn a lot of his money on himself: the Versace shirt, the gold chain, the Rolex watch. And to top it off, there was no one there to pick him up because he'd thought he could just *show up* in Najia.

Bosco had never laughed as hard as he had that day. He also never understood why Nigerians living abroad needed to announce their newfound wealth with expensive clothing and appurtenances. He thought the entire exercise unnecessary since just their skin showed better living. The little times Bosco went on social media, he noticed that the average Nigerian in Nigeria had a different silent disposition about them than the Nigerian living abroad. For instance, Bosco thought there was a certain sheen of desperation that coated the skin of the average Nigerian at home like a moisturizer, despite the tropical weather the country was blessed with.

When Bosco saw Ken with all the designers he was wearing, Bosco had pitied him. Here was a guy *begging* to be victimized. Bosco's military training and years of putting the needs and image of his country ahead of himself had overwhelmed him with pity for the young man. Bosco had approached him and offered to arrange a ride for him. Ken had naively agreed. They'd formed a connection. Bosco would later educate Ken on the errors of his wardrobe and *borrow him some sense* on how to conduct himself in Nigeria. Thinking he'd found a guide of sorts, Ken had called Bosco up the next day to take him around Lagos. And when Ken relocated to Nigeria a few years later, Bosco had been one of the first people he'd called to work for him.

Bosco believed it was his job to keep his boss's secrets and to keep his boss safe. And he took that two-pronged commitment very seriously. And in all his years of doing just that, with all the comings and goings he'd seen – and he'd seen bribery of public officials, teaching unruly club patrons some lessons, girlfriends that got too clingy, girlfriends that arrived before side-chicks left – he'd only seen Ken truly bothered twice: the first was after madam Lisa broke things off with him and the second was now. He'd seen Ken take a phone call that lasted about a minute or two shortly after Ije's departure. Then he'd seen him sit at his desk and just stare into space, breathing heavily. First, Bosco had thought Ken was having an asthma attack, but Ken had waved off the inhaler Bosco offered, which was the only movement Ken had made in the last few minutes.

"Boss, is everything okay? You're not looking alright o," Bosco repeated.

Ken slowly got up from his desk and said, "Take me to Lisa," in a dreamlike state.

The drive to LUTH did not change Ken's demeanor. He sat transfixed in the back passenger seat, not paying any attention to anything Bosco was saying. Whatever the news was that Ken had received, it must have been really bad.

When they got to LUTH, Ken did not call Lisa or get out of the car. He just sat there. Bosco was very worried. He hurriedly went in search of Lisa and relayed to her all that he could from his limited vantage point. He could not tell her what his boss had heard or why his boss had stopped speaking since.

When Lisa opened the door to where Ken was seating in his Bentley, she could see what had Bosco worried: Ken was in quiet panic. Lisa could see the panic in the rapid movement of his eyes, but he wasn't moving much or saying anything to her.

"Ken, what happened? Are you okay?"

That seemed to jolt Ken somewhat. "My mom."

"What happened to your mom?"

"She had a stroke."

"Oh." Lisa took a moment to gather herself. "Okay. Have you gone to see her? Where is she?"

Ken looked at her with terror-filled eyes. "She's in UCH in Ibadan."

Ken could not bring himself to go see his mom. His mom's primary care doctor had called from University College Hospital in Ibadan and directed Ken to make his way to Ibadan right away.

Lisa hurriedly called Sylvia to let her know she was headed to Ibadan. Still with her white coat, Lisa got in the car and the three headed to Ibadan.

**

You mom didn't just have a stroke.

The voice behind those words sounded very distant, though the doctors were standing mere feet away from Ken where he was seated next to his mom's rested body. Lisa was the one talking to the team of doctors, Since Ken couldn't get himself to say anything.

Ken was having trouble processing seeing his mom like *this*. Nigerian moms were a whole vibe, but his mom had double the vibe dose for days. She was the life of every party, every gathering. His mom was never sick, never downcast. He'd seen her cry only twice his entire life: when his younger sister died and then again when his dad died. And when his younger sister had died, his mom had cried – more like screamed in agony – at the initial hearing of the news. But when she saw him and his dad start to cry, she'd stopped, stood up straighter and began to comfort *them*. She'd later channeled all her grief towards keeping him safe from anything she thought could harm him, though he'd not given her a lot of rest in that regard. But when his dad died, she'd cried a lot. Not when *he* cried had she comforted him. She'd been inconsolable. It was like she'd felt hopeless. That was why Ken had been glad when she relocated to Nigeria to be closer to her family and old school friends. She'd seemed to have rediscovered a reason to live. And he'd been happy for her. This…*this* stretched and seemingly lifeless body in front of him was not *his* mother. He didn't recognize this person with swollen eyes and tubes coming in and out of her. Her eyes looked like she'd been in a street fight and been punched several times.

"Why are her eyes swollen?" Ken asked, interrupting the discussing team of doctors without taking his eyes of his mom, without letting go of her hand, without stopping his soft caress of the one spot on the back of her hand that was not pierced through with a needle.

"Periorbital edema. Facial swelling and proptosis – " said one of the doctors before Lisa interrupted him.

"Why don't we continue this discussion in your office, Dr. Bayowa," Lisa said before Ken vociferated a loud, "No!"

Lisa thanked the team of doctors and made plans to confer with them later, while Ken stayed where he was beside his mom. He felt fear course through him as he took in the sight before him. His mom was his last living immediate family member. Ken considered himself a self-assured and confident man; some may even say he was arrogant, but facing the sudden loss of his last close relative was a cruel gut-punch. And Ken was reeling. As much as he hated passing his burdens to Lisa, the prospect before him was too daunting for him.

"Tell me about your mom, Ken. I want to meet her through you," Lisa's soft voice pierced his thoughts.

It was a few moments before Ken began to speak, his eyes still trained on his mom. "She was the shortest in her family…but if she was small, she didn't know it. She had a Napoleon complex for days. The first problem my mom couldn't solve was mine and my sister's asthma. Anything else, she took it head on and conquered it. Her spirit was indomitable. She was a proud Igbo woman."

"You're going to beat this, too, mom," Ken began to address his mom directly. "I know you will. This is *nothing* for you. You're going to pull through. You *have* to. You need to meet Lisa. I know I've told you about *her*, but you have to meet her yourself."

Ken continued to talk to his mom about Lisa, oblivious to the departure of the same Lisa.

Lisa quietly exited the room. She didn't want to be privy to a conversation that wasn't meant for her ears. Ken talking to his mom was good enough for now. Lisa didn't hear Ken profess his love for her to his mom. She didn't hear him tell his mom that he'd found his own strong Igbo-Yoruba woman, that Lisa was the love of his life.

Lisa stepped out into the hallway and walked a few steps before leaning against the wall to collect herself. The prognosis was bad – Cerebral Venous Sinus Thrombosis. It was an extremely rare occurrence that accompanied a stroke. Blood stopped draining from the brain and the accumulation caused bleeding in the brain. It is what caused facial edema and her swollen eyes. Somehow, Mrs. Amadi had had several silent strokes without knowing it. What she'd thought was a headache was not just a headache. This last stroke had been followed by seizures, resulting in the state she was currently in.

Lisa looked down at her left hand. It was shaking ever so slightly. She balled it into a fist then released the fist to stop the shaking. She'd been doing that a lot lately. Not since first year of surgery in medical school when Lisa had to deal with a horrible professor who almost shattered her self-confidence had her hand shaken this much. Lisa had achieved surgery grade steady hands with the help of someone dear to her back in medical school. Her left hand was shaking now because she was unsure about a lot of things. And the lack of certainty made her nervous, which further complicated the lack of certainty. And all of *that* didn't include the volatility of her situationship with Ken. They were not a couple, yet here she was. When she'd seen him in that near-catatonic state, *nothing* could have stopped her from going to the ends of the world or walking through hell with him; it just had not occurred to her to turn Ken away.

"Ada?"

The voice dragged Lisa back to the present, jarring her out of her thoughts. Only one person called her 'Ada.' And she recognized the mesmerizing voice in its baritone richness, a voice that sang worship songs just as it sang many love songs to Lisa in the past, a voice that she'd fallen completely in love with as a young impressionable pre-med student at Uni-Ibadan.

CHAPTER FIVE

"Dr. Bakre." Lisa could hardly believe she was in the presence of Bankole Bakre – her first love. Banks, as everyone called him, was the reason for a lot of who and what Lisa was. What had started as a mentor-mentee relationship, which her faculty advisor – Dr. Ajanaku – had thought would be very good for Lisa since she'd entered university at such a young age, had gradually morphed into a romantic one.

Banks was Dr. Ajanaku's nephew and many years older than Lisa. His parents lived in the UK where Banks had finished his medical studies. He'd come to Nigeria for another residency at the prestigious UCH as part of his global aspirations in the medical profession. Banks was the gorgeous boy next door. His six-foot frame was that of sprinter, lean and muscled. And his dreadlocks added a depth to him. Lisa's favorite thing about Banks had been how his eyes twinkled when something amused him. If a lady was lucky enough to amuse him, he'd bestow the glory of his perfect dentition on her. And here was Banks in front of Lisa, looking better than ever.

"I didn't know you were back."

"*Ca fait des jour*, Ada," Banks commented on how long it had been since they last saw each other. "I tried reaching you but you must have changed your number? *C'est comment? Tu bara dans isi?*" lapsing in and out of French, Banks asked about Lisa's wellbeing and if she was working in UCH.

"Not at all. I came with a -" Lisa caught herself as she responded in English and started again, "I came to see a patient, but I'll be heading back to Lagos shortly. I have a clinic in Lagos."

"Wow. Dr. Ada. Look at you. All grown up. It is so good to see you again. Let's catch up, won't you?"

"Aren't you married, Banks?" Lisa was not one for useless small talk.

"No, I'm not. Nothing has worked out with anyone else."

This was where most people would say something nice. Well, Lisa didn't lie.

"Well, sometimes it doesn't," Lisa said with uncharacteristic hurry. "But you look well. Take care!" She moved to go as Banks reached for her hand, which Lisa withdrew, but not before he saw the barely noticeable shaking. A knowing look passed between the two before Banks gently let her hand go.

"Let's catch up, Ada, please. I'd really like us to. There are some things I'd like to discuss with you...about the way things ended between us...and I do owe you an apology, Ada. Several apologies."

Lisa wondered at what Banks wanted to apologize for. Though things hadn't ended well between them, Lisa had never blamed Banks for it. He'd wanted to pursue global aspirations. She hadn't. And they'd parted ways. Though Lisa had loved Banks deeply, she'd not considered, even for a moment, giving up her own dreams for him. With that resolve, Lisa had known it was a matter of time for her heart to follow her brain and let Banks go. For Lisa, it had been that simple. Still, she was curious. Sylvia believed that the reason why Lisa couldn't seem to get over Ken had something to do with Banks. Sylvia believed that Ken was Lisa's overcorrection of the relationship mistakes she'd made with Banks. For that reason alone, Lisa wanted to meet with Banks. Perhaps there was something to this closure thing after all.

"Okay. Here's my number. And Banks? I go by Lisa or Dr. Lisa now," she said, turned around with a pronounced whip of her hair.

Ken kept to himself on the drive back to Lagos on the Expressway. He considered that the distance it took to cover this same stretch of road was less than the daily commute of some Americans, especially the ones who lived in suburbs but worked in adjacent cities. Still, the journey on the Expressway was prolonged and complicated by gridlock and bad road conditions. Much like the road of life, where outcomes are heavily influenced by events people experience and how they process those events. Ije came to his mind. It was easy for others, including himself, to judge Ije's choices, but very few would survive what Ije has survived: dealing with the death of both parents at a very young age; sent to live with an uncle – her only other relative – who turned out to be a lewd and disgusting, wide open asshole who couldn't keep his hands off his pubescent niece; running away to survive on the streets of Lagos. Any one of those events would indelibly mark any other person; but Ije continued to thrive her own way and chart her own course. She refused to be a victim of life; he *had* to respect her for it.

It was more than he could say for himself. Here he was, no better than a sulking kid. He couldn't even bring himself to talk to Lisa who was sitting right next to him. He'd been staring out the window since they left UCH. He had not said much of anything to Lisa since they both left his mom's room. Although, he'd seen her chat with some guy in the hallway and he'd wondered who *he* was and why he was being too familiar with Lisa. Though Ken was only mere inches away from Lisa, he felt entirely removed from her and completely alone. Ken did not want to place his burdens on anyone, let alone Lisa. She was not his burden bearer. He'd done enough dragging her on an unplanned trip to Ibadan.

Ken reached in his pants pocket for his inhaler while continuing to stare out the window from his side of the back seat. The Expressway gridlock meant an overabundance of carbon monoxide puffing and oozing from the exhaust pipes of vehicles that were not road-worthy. As he absent-mindedly rested his hands on the space between himself and Lisa after taking the customary two puffs of his inhaler, he felt her hand close over his. That was when he realized he'd balled both hands into tight fists. He looked at where their hands connected and then up at Lisa. She looked at him with...understanding and presence. She didn't say a word, yet he heard a lot. He heard it was okay for him to be silent, but she would listen if he wanted to talk. He heard that she cared. And that was enough for Ken as he opened his hand to hold hers. It was enough to snap him out of his toxic train of thought.

***

Lisa extended an invitation to Ken to come inside as she was dropped her off at her parents'. Despite their differences, Lisa knew that her parents would want to pray with Ken about his mom. Still, Ken declined her invitation, opting for he and Bosco to head straight home. Lisa soon found out that Ken's decline of her invitation was for the best. Pastor Dare was not in the mood to entertain this unforeseen guest.

"I thought you'd stopped seeing him, my love," Pastor Dare's gentle inquisition betrayed no turmoil inside.

"Dad, out of everything I just told you, that's the only thing you heard?"

"Heard *and* saw. He dropped you off here…at this time of the night. And I am just asking why you two would be together at this time of the night."

"We came back late from Ibadan. His mom is very sick, Dad. Ken could use a friend right now, and I am not going to let him go through this alone."

It wasn't lost on Lisa that her mom had not said much. Pastor Chi was quietly moving through the house without joining the conversation, which was surprising to Lisa. The Pastor Chi that Lisa knew was vocal in her disapproval of Ken.

"Time plus words equal intimacy," Pastor Dare continued, sharing the formula he was famous for amongst the singles at BESEM. "It doesn't matter if your intention is only to be friends. If you are spending time with him, especially as he is going through difficulty, you are building intimacy with him. You are setting yourself up, my love. So, if you're done with this man, leave him alone and let him go," Pastor Dare warned.

"His mom is *very* sick, Dad," Lisa repeated. "Whatever happened to caring for the sick? Isn't that what Jesus would want us to do?"

"And I am sure his mother has a great team of doctors who are helping her. *We* can pray for him and her, but that is it."

"Kene," Pastor Chi finally spoke.

"What?" Pastor Dare responded, not quite understanding Pastor Chi's one-word contribution.

"His name is Kenechukwu. You can't even say his name, Dare."

Dare? What's going on right now? Lisa thought to herself as she observed both her parents. Her mom almost never called her dad by his first name unless she was flirting or angry, both of which were usually out of their children's sight.

"Chiamaka, not right now," Pastor Dare stated defiantly. Something else that Lisa could count the number of times she'd witnessed.

"What's going on with you two?" Lisa asked them.

"Mind your business," they responded simultaneously.

"This *is* my business. We are talking about Ken. And Dad? Mom is right. He has a name."

"My business with him has concluded. I don't need to learn his name or build any relationship with him. But I promise you that I will be praying for his mother...and for him."

"Kene," Pastor Chi repeated, "we will be praying for Kene and his mother. But like your father said, Adaolisa, you must be intentional about what you are doing with this man."

"That's not what I said, Chiamaka. Don't put words in my mouth."

"Okay, that's what *I* am saying," Pastor Chi countered her husband before continuing, "Because the last thing you want is to find yourself in a place where you don't want to go. If you've decided there is no future for you and Kene, don't fool yourself by being *friends*; that is foolishness."

Lisa stared at her mother askance. It almost sounded like Pastor Chi was backing off her disapproval of Ken? *Something else must have happened,* Lisa thought to herself as she continued to stare at her mom.

"Okaaaay," Lisa nodded.

"Look, Adaolisa," Pastor Chi continued, "Don't overwork that your head trying to figure anything out. I am praying about this, and I am counseling you. But I also know that the way of a man with a woman is mysterious. That's what the Bible says. As parents, all we can do is to guide our children with wisdom and prayers. If you choose what you choose, know that you cannot choose the consequences of your choice," Pastor Chi submitted with her shoulder shrug.

"We are just friends," Lisa reiterated to Pastor Dare's amusement.

"Adaolisa, there is no such thing. A man can *never* be just friends with a woman he wants. You better know and accept that fact," Pastor Dare countered.

"I disagree with you, Dad."

"Okay. I don't want to argue with you. We will continue to pray for his mother…and him, too."

CHAPTER SIX

"I think it's a really good idea, Lisa," Sylvia said as the ladies went for a neighborhood jog, indicating her agreement with Bank's suggestion to catch up with Lisa.

"Of course, you do, Sylvia. What else is new? You've always been Banks' biggest cheerleader."

"Yes, I do think you and Banks make more sense than *that* other guy, but that's not the point. I think you haven't fully resolved you and Banks."

Sylvia knew the history of *'A&B'* – the moniker given to Adaolisa and Banks as soon as their relationship went social-media-official – very well. Assignment of university hostels was usually based on student tenure; so, it was not at all unusual for more tenured post-graduation medical students to have their choice of the selection. Banks had not only had his pick of hostels, but he'd also been able to afford a *boy's quarters* – BQ, as they're called – in one of the professors' official residences. What had been unusual, however, was for a post-graduate medical resident, one as popular as Banks had been, to make his BQ available for campus fellowships.

Banks had been a big man on campus; the combination of his looks, that British accent that peeked through, respected course of study and involvement in campus fellowships, had made him known and popular to virtually every demographic that mattered on campus. Even the underbellies of campus respected him and knew to leave him alone. After all, his uncle had enough pull and clout to rusticate any student that egregiously violated the code of conduct; and cultism was considered an egregious violation.

Banks had been one hundred yards of pure husband material, the imported kind. Every blessed recipient of his perfect smile had considered him a potential husband; and the ones who hadn't had been either blind or already married to Jesus. Even the blind ones asked their seeing companions for a description as soon as they heard his baritone voice. His BQ apartment had been cool, too. With the internationally connected media set and opportunity to chill with any preferred streaming service provider, a makeshift office area comprised of a desk and his laptop, an acoustic guitar propped up against the wall, a fridge that worked and was usually full of the foods his rich aunties sent to him, and cupboards filled with provisions, his BQ had been the perfect hangout.

Being Lisa's course mentor, Banks had met with Lisa weekly. At first, Banks had simply been a big brother to her, a really smart one. Lisa had marveled at not just the extent of his knowledge of medicine, but also his international exposure to the practice of medicine. Whenever Lisa had course-related questions, Banks would give theoretical answers and practical examples based on his experience, as well as pointers for further research. It was fair to say that Banks had been instrumental to Lisa's success as a medical student. Slowly, professional admiration had morphed into admiration of a more personal kind. Lisa had initially put it off to a schoolgirl crush, and she'd refused to embarrass herself and Banks by even hinting at her feelings for him. But after she'd caught several longing glances, she'd known her crush was crushing, too.

"There's nothing to resolve with Banks. We'll just be catching up," Lisa responded to Sylvia. "Banks and Ken are so….different…although both very *fine*."

"Whoa, gist me! How is brother doctor Banks looking these days," Sylvia said with an exaggerated shoulder shimmy. "Is he still as…um…well-sculpted by the hand of God Almighty?"

"Better-looking," Lisa admitted, playfully feeding fodder to Sylvia's curiosity.

"How?! He's not fat and balding?"

"Actually, I think he's hair line may have gotten fuller," Lisa faked reflectiveness.

"How is that even possible?"

"Babes, I didn't believe it until I saw it myself."

Both ladies laughed before Sylvia continued, "You should *definitely* catch up with him. Who knows…," she trailed off.

"Sylvia, *you* know there's no way forward there. You know why Banks and I broke up, *had to* break up."

"He's back in Nigeria! Maybe his global aspirations have changed."

"Doubt it."

"Why? He was *parleying Francais* again?"

"Yup."

"Wow! A Christian brother who can talk in other tongues. Me likey!"

Lisa laughed at her friend's antics as the pair slowed their jog down. Sylvia was that common-sense, matter-of-fact Christian who didn't think every problem was caused by village people's voodoo, and people needed to take more personal responsibility for their bad behaviors. Her worldview was to ask God for help, knowing God expected her to do what He already gave her hands and legs to do.

"Listen, you should find the person you're dating or considering for marriage attractive. It's just common sense."

"You can't base a relationship on attraction alone, though," Lisa retorted weakly, thinking more about what she currently felt for Ken and how that was not enough, would never be enough, to build a relationship. "With Banks, everything else checked out, but I can't drop it all and follow him around the world."

"Dr. *medicine sans frontier. Le bleu, le bleu, le bleu bleu bleu...bleu,*" Sylvia exaggerated a French accent.

Lisa herself could carry a basic conversation in French because Banks had spoken it to her so often as their relationship became more exclusive. French with Ivoirian dialect was one of the seven languages Banks spoke fluently due to his family ties to Abidjan by way of Ejigbo.

The Bakres were Ivoirians who had migrated to Ejigbo in the early 1900s. Banks' great grandfather had acquired land in the Ejigbo town of Osun State where he'd farmed. His son – Bankole's grandfather – had continued with farming. While Bankole's grandfather had died in Ejigbo, he'd told his son – Bankole's father – to ensure he was buried among his family in Cote d'Ivoire. Bankole's father had obliged *his* father, moving his family back to Abijdan just as the third decade of President Felix Houphouet Boigny of Cote d'Ivoire's tenure in office began. Bankole's father had heard stories of good times rolling in during President Boigny's tenure from the family he'd traced to Abidjan. After the family moved to Abidjan in the late seventies, they'd lived there for another ten or so years.

The Bakres claim both countries equally, having family houses in both Nigeria and Cote d'Ivoire. Though all eight children born to Bankole's grandfather had been working-class, they'd also been professionals at the highest level of their chosen fields. Beyond their formal education, however, the Bakres were cosmopolitans, usually well-traveled and informed on happenings around the world. Their pattern was always the same: the Bakres did early childhood education in Nigeria, then travelled to some other country in Europe or the Americas.

But as they say, home was always the farmer's destination, and home was in Ejigbo for the Bakres.

Bankole was the last of four children and the only one born outside Africa. His parents brought seven-year-old Bankole back to Nigeria for his early education and left him with extended family in Ibadan. His childhood was rich with memories made with cousins, aunties and uncles from Ibadan and Abidjan. Bankole had stayed back in Nigeria for secondary education and only returned to United Kingdom for his tertiary education. Since he'd wanted his post-graduate studies in medicine to be among the West Africans he ultimately wanted to serve, he'd returned home after graduating from university.

Though Banks had also learned Parisian French while in the United Kingdom, he'd rejected what he termed the rigidity of the phonetics and pronunciation, preferring the pizzaz and flirtatiousness of Ivoirian French. French was the language of his heart, he'd say. And he'd spoken French to Lisa often because she mattered to his heart.

"All I'm saying is if Ken and his sinful ways hadn't come into the picture, you'd be on baby number 15 with Dr. Banks."

"Pretty much. I'd be barefoot, pregnant every nine months."

"And it's not too late. Go get your happy, babe!"

"Sylvia, 15 babies and trotting after some guy isn't what I pictured for my life. With all the boxes Banks checked, I didn't see myself in his future plans."

"Forget your life! *Who your life epp*? Listen, let me borrow you some Delilah slash Ruth sense here. Go get your Boaz and if you have to lay at his feet or he needs to rest his handsome head on your thighs, do what you gotta do, babes.

"Wow. Where are those Christian morals now?"

"Look, it is hot *and cold* out here for righteous single ladies. And you got a *perfect* guy and you're here telling me he doesn't fit into your life. You need to hurry up and make up your mind."

"I want to be more than *just* wife. Banks wants *just* wife. I don't doubt that he'll make a good husband, but not for me."

It was the same old story: daughters judging their mother's choices too harshly and vowing not to turn out like their mothers, thinking they would have made different choices if they'd been in their mothers' shoes. And maybe there was some truth to that. But that didn't change the fact that in Lisa's case,

Sylvia thought Lisa was wrong. Pastor Chi was living a blissfully happy life while snatching souls from the gates of hell.

"Lisa, not wanting to be your mom is a bad way to live your life. It usually has the opposite effect, I'm telling you. Besides, do you hear Pastor Chi complaining?"

"Pastor Chi could have been a medical doctor, Sylvia! She gave it up for a man. I will never understand that."

"Hmmm… This is you thinking you can do it better *abi?* All I know is, Pastor Chi is living her best life. Do the same with yours and stop trying to right an imaginary wrong. For that date or catch-up or whatever, make sure you're dressed well, not like that nonsense you wore to your date with Ken. Dress to remind Dr. Banks of what he *could* taste again if he played his cards right and put a ring on it."

"Chai! For a man, you are ready to lay down your salvation."

"Correction: a saved, Christian man."

"Wow. Well, I will *not* be following your advice. I will probably go in my work clothes."

"You will do no such thing. I forbid it," Sylvia called after Lisa as they walked the rest of the way back to their apartment.

CHAPTER SEVEN

Lisa met Banks at the suya spot in her work clothes: scrubs, white coat and a stethoscope around her neck to complete the look. She could have gone home to change but she'd opted not to. She'd worked till the last possible minute. Whether it was a date or just old friends catching up, she didn't care; and she knew Banks wouldn't care either. Banks had known her when she was a bumbling medical student with a head full of theoretical knowledge and nothing else.

Banks was the one who had helped Lisa achieve surgery grade steady hands. *"Y'a rien, C'est propre,"* had been his encouraging refrain, even though she'd been sure her technique had been far from perfect. Other times, Banks would quote the Bible to her, *"God makes you surefooted as a deer...God trains your hands for battle."* Lisa's self-assured confidence had gradually paired with her superior theoretical knowledge of medicine to earn the praise and respect of instructors and colleagues.

But before Banks became her mentor, *suya* had been Lisa's only best friend. That pathetically delicious relationship continued throughout her first year of college and until Banks and Sylvia came into the picture.

Bank wrote her poetry that poured from deep within him. He'd cook her meals when she was studying for finals and too tired to nourish herself properly. And when she'd been frustrated, he would play her music on his acoustic guitar. As first loves go, theirs had been perfect. They spent every possible moment together, too much time together. It hadn't mattered that some of those times were spent side by side in silence. That had been one of the oddest things about them. Because they both always had their noses buried in some medical textbook or the other, it had been perfectly normal for them to study different things side by side. Without much effort, Lisa had fallen hard for Banks and Banks had done the same. And perhaps that is where the caution of wisdom rooted in their faith should have set in, but it hadn't. Inevitably, their budding emotional intimacy had segued to intimacy of a more physical kind. Even then, Lisa had not minded; she'd felt no dissonance due to the incongruity of an active sex life and involvement in campus fellowship. The way she'd seen it, she would eventually marry Banks; everything else was formality.

Banks had not seen it the same way. The guilt had eaten him alive. His zeal as a new believer had made his inability to control his body around Lisa very difficult to reconcile. Eventually, Banks had found a reason to distance himself from Lisa: he wanted to travel for a while. Lisa could either marry him and come with him as his wife or they would need to end things. Lisa hated the ultimatum and declined the offer. She would, under no earthly or otherworldly circumstance, do the same thing her mother did by leaving school to trot after a guy. She'd broken it off.

"Tu n'aimes plus suya? You're not eating," Banks questioned, inquiring if something was wrong with Lisa's food or she no longer loved *suya.* Lost in thought, Lisa had been pushing her *suya* back and forth since the pair had been served.

"No, it's fine."

"Did you come here from work?"

"Yes. Busy day. I didn't go home to change." Lisa figured Banks may feel a type of way at her lack of effort at her appearance.

"Non, tu es sape," Banks complimented Lisa's appearance. "It doesn't matter what you wear, Lisa."

Lisa didn't acknowledge or respond to the compliment.

"So, Dr. Lisa," Banks continued. *"On dit quoi? Tu fais rien avec moi."* (What's up? You forgot about me).

"That's usually what happens after breakup," Lisa responded cheekily.

"D'accord, d'accord. I'm glad to see you're well."

Lisa asked him about his international travels and work around Africa. And Dr. Bankole Bakre had a lot to say. He'd worked on ships filled with other volunteer medical professionals as they sailed around the world to provide life-saving intervention. He'd worked with organizations that provided aid to war-torn countries. He'd also spent some of his time in the remotest parts of Nigeria, helping to set up preventative care clinics and to organize donations.

Lisa shared her work with Mama Abiye with Banks, and her plans to build a clinic that provided care to low-income Lagosians. Banks gave her information on international organizations and big-name donors to help with the funding.

It seemed the pair were not only catching up, but they were also discovering that their paths may be coinciding after all. Though Lisa wanted to remain in Nigeria and Banks's ambition was to touch the world with the love of God through medicine, their premise was the same – care for the underprivileged. That had always been something they both valued.

Banks also shared that though he'd had a few relationships, nothing had worked as well as him and Lisa. Banks had returned to Nigeria fully intentioned to find Lisa. Meeting at UCH, Banks believed, had been a god-wink. He was single and looking to pick up with her where they'd left off.

Lisa didn't say a word about Ken.

"And how is the patient you came to see in UCH doing?"

"Not very well. The diagnosis is CSVT."

"Ca c'est tres mauvais. Are they related to you?"

"Not really. Mom of a friend."

"Yako," Banks expressed sympathy. "Would surgical intervention be too risky?"

"Yeah. There are comorbidities. The patient is also advanced in age, history of controlled asthma…"

Lisa still hadn't said a word about her personal connection to the patient. She wouldn't have to. Lost in their shoptalk, neither paid attention to the owner of the restaurant who had just walked in, looking worn and tired.

Ken had spotted Lisa's car outside. His heart had leapt to his throat at the thought that he was about to see her. But when he saw her sitting across some guy and it became clear that they were on a date, Ken's leaping heart settled back into its position as he slowly walked up to the pair and stood by their table.

"Hello Ken," Lisa greeted him. "This is my friend, Bankole Bakre. Dr. Banks and I were at UCH together."

"Hello, Ken. Nice to meet you, Brother" Banks greeted as he politely stood and extended his hand to Ken.

***

Brother. He's one of those, Ken thought to himself. Ken had seen the guy before. He was the same guy talking to Lisa in UCH, only he'd thought Banks was one of the attending physicians. No wonder Banks had been too close to Lisa for Ken's comfort. Now Ken knew why: the guy was also *attending his* Lisa, it would seem.

And the nerve of Lisa, bringing this guy here. To his place! Was her plan to make him jealous or what mind game was Lisa playing? Surely, she knew he routinely checked on his spot. Ken didn't take the hand Banks offered. He looked at Lisa, looked at the guy, looked at the extended hand again and walked away towards the kitchen area.

His retreating figure heard Lisa apologize to the guy on his behalf.

Much later, Ken was rifling through papers on the desk of his manager as Lisa barged into the back office.

"Can I help you?" Ken said to Lisa who was obviously fuming. *She is angry?!* Ken thought to himself.

"Yes, as a matter of fact, you can. What was that about? Why were you so rude to Banks?" Lisa asked.

"Okay, so this is you telling me to be nicer to your *boyfriend*? Noted. Anything else?" Ken was dismissing her as he continued to look through papers.

"I don't understand what the attitude is about. You and I are just friends, right? What's with the attitude?"

"Lisa, I am not your *friend*. I will *never* be your friend. Maybe homeboy over there is okay with being *just friends.* Not me. And the nerve of you bringing him to *my* place. You couldn't find anywhere else?"

"I didn't know there was a preapproval process for your patrons."

Ken didn't respond to the sarcastic quip. Instead, he said, "He's the one you slept with, isn't it?" Ken stated, more than asked.

"None of your business, Ken! I don't ask you about your past. Who do you think you are!?"

Ken paused before saying, "I shouldn't have asked that. You're right; it's none of my business," Ken apologized. But there was that unease in his gut that told him he didn't mean the apology. And Lisa was glaring at him for his brazenly rude question. "You know what, I take the apology back. I am *not* sorry. You want to know the people I've slept with? Because I'll tell you!"

"I don't want to know. That's your business!"

"I'm making it yours! Ask away."

"Not necessary. Why, so you can pry into mine? Not going to happen, Ken. Dr. Banks is a friend I hold in very high esteem. That's all you need to know."

Ken laughed wryly. He considered Lisa one of the smartest people he'd ever met; yet, there were some things she didn't seem to know about life. Or perhaps she knew but was too naïve to accept that those things were the way they were. Like the fact that men and women cannot be *just friends*. Even more so, a woman can never be just friends with an ex she'd slept with.

"Homeboy is not some guy off the street. You have history with him and you are currently on a date with him. At *my* place. And I'm supposed to be okay with that?"

"Not that it would excuse your behavior towards Banks, but you have no rights to me, Ken. We are just friends. Being friends with you doesn't mean I can't have other friends. I can be friends with whomever I choose, including Banks."

"Lisa, a guy cannot be *just friends* with a woman he's slept with. It's impossible."

"In your world, maybe. Not in mine." Lisa's disagreement was vehement and steady. She clearly thought Ken's perspective on the subject was archaic and ridiculous. "How come you and I are friends? We've been *just friends* for months now."

"You just proved my point! I very much want to sleep with you…very soon." Ken said with a satisfied smirk on his face. "Lisa, let me break it down for you. *No guy* wants to hear your life problems and help you solve them unless he's getting something in return or he is your father. Any guy who tells you otherwise is just lounging in that friendzone as a – and forgive the expression – a dick in a box."

"What on earth is a dick in a box?" Lisa asked with incredulity.

"I'm glad you asked," Ken continued with mock seriousness. "A dick in a box is like a toy. And that *toy* is hoping that with the right alignment of the stars, you will take it out of the box and play with it. That's why *brother* Banks over there didn't turn you down when the stars aligned just right for you two. Accept it or not, it's the way it is, Lisa."

Based on Lisa's reaction, Ken could see she was flummoxed by his reference and conviction.

"Wow. That is perhaps the worst commentary I have ever heard on male-female relationships. And I disagree with you completely. Are you saying you are just waiting to sleep with all *your* female friends?"

"Yes," Ken responded deadpan. "That's why I don't have any. You are my only female *friend*. Any other female I know are acquaintances necessary to some purposeful end. I don't like tormenting myself. I don't pursue any type of relationship with them, platonic or anything deeper. Been there, done that and it cost me too much."

He was referring to the fiasco with Ije. He could see Lisa knew, too. Lisa said she'd forgiven Ken, but it didn't seem that her forgiveness included reconciliation.

"Do you want to talk about her?" Ken asked, referring to Ije.

"Not necessary."

If there was one thing Ken learned from the burning of Adagio, it was to walk away when there was no way. Protracting a defeat usually leads to greater defeat. The stubborn businessman in him wanted to find a way and fight back. He'd never wanted anything as much as he wanted to marry Lisa and build a life with her. She was his loftiest, highest desire. Yet, the weight those two words carried hit Ken like a ton of bricks. Ken knew in that moment that Lisa's silence on what happened with Ije is exactly what her silence always means: there was something negative she didn't want to say.

"You really don't think there's a future for us, do you." It wasn't a question. He simply stated it and prayerfully hoped she would deny it. This woman standing in front of him, taller than her petite frame, looking at and through him simultaneously, did not want to tell him that she didn't give second chances.

He waited for her to deny it.

She didn't.

"We can be *just* friends, Ken," Lisa said after more silence.

"Like you and brother dark-and-lovely?" Ken let out a mirthless laugh. The guy looked like the type of person who would agree to being just friends.

Ken fantasized about the many ways he could hurt the first guy who settled for the friendzone. The best available alternative for a man whose mind was set on more primitive agenda surely was not to hold hands, braid pigtails or whatever the hell else *besties* did. *What guy worth his salt would settle for that!?* Ken thought to himself.

"Ace?" Ken said with deliberate intentionality. "I'm sorry but I don't want to be your *friend*. From the first day I met you, it never crossed my mind that this girl would be my *friend*. You've plagued my thoughts and dreams in the most *unfriendly* way, and the more I know you the more attracted I am to you. I have never wanted a woman like I want you. And what makes it…um… more difficult is I realize this is not just about sex. Do you know that? Do you know that I have not had anything even close to sex since the night you walked in on me and Ije? Because the thought of another woman is immediately interrupted by you. You're all I want, the only one I want. I want you more because I want to show you how I feel the best way I know. And I have never felt this way about anyone. It is driving me more insane with every waking day. Do you get that?"

"I get it," Lisa responded reluctantly.

"I don't think so. If you did, you would know how ridiculous I find being just friends with you."

In that moment, the seeming impossibility of the situation frustrated both equally. The months of sniffing around each other did not help. Ken's lips met Lisa's. This was not a kiss for a friend. This kiss was a promise and a prayer. A promise of possibilities and the prayer of desperate man. With his kiss, Ken sought to convince Lisa beyond his words, that there was no scenario in which they ended up as friends. Lisa didn't argue with the conviction of Ken's kisses. In fact, she pliantly kissed him back with equal ardor.

Ken spoke first after breaking the kiss as he whispered, "I don't want to be your friend. And if there was any doubt in my mind before, the way you kissed me back erased it. You don't want to be just friends either. So, be my girl, Ace."

"Attraction fades, Ken."

"Don't trivialize us that way. You know this is more than just attraction, Lisa."

"What is it? What is it if it's not just attraction?"

"There's something about me you can't ignore, Lisa! I know that because I know you've tried, yet here you are. Do you realize I have never gotten your voicemail? You always pick up when I call. As busy as you are. It doesn't matter if you're angry with me, hate me or if anything else is going on. You always pick up," Ken pleaded in desperation. "I feel the same way, too. I can't... shake this *shit*! Christian or not, you have to work at a good marriage. I saw my parents do it and you've seen yours do it. Marry me, Lisa, and let's go to work. He may check all the boxes, but that guy is not who you want. You want me."

"Ken, I...I... think we need to not see each other for a while," Lisa said without meeting Ken's face. "With everything else going on with your mom, I don't think it's good to complicate your life with whatever this is. And I need a clear head, too."

"So you can restart things with *him?*"

Lisa didn't answer. She didn't need to.

CHAPTER EIGHT

Abundant foliage and soothing sounds of falling waters made IITA – International Institute of Tropical Agriculture – a favorite date spot for those who had access. One could never tell the direction of the waterfall – if there was a waterfall– but the sounds were all around the meandering walkways, from the cafeteria to the tennis court and the pool. The ambience offered a calm serenity for a quiet, almost contemplative socializing.

Lisa and Banks loved coming to IITA back in their university days. Coming to IITA meant they could enjoy a romantic evening without spending too much money. They'd wander the walkways, simply enjoying each other's company. One such stroll led to Lisa's first kiss.

Lisa travelled to Ibadan to see Ken's mom a few days after her date at the *suya* spot with one man had ended with her kissing another man. Perhaps she shouldn't have asked Banks to meet her at one of Ken's businesses for a date; but Lisa had honestly thought Ken would be in Ibadan with his mom or some other place. Lisa didn't believe she'd asked to meet there in hopes of running into Ken and making him jealous. She didn't want to believe she could be that petty. Only her pettiness had backfired. *That kiss…*

Lisa considered that it was hard for Ken to imagine a world where *he* wasn't the center of her world. But there had been a time when she worshipped the ground Banks walked on and thought every word out of his mouth was honey. One kiss from Ken and all she'd ever felt or experienced with Banks felt as tepid as handholding. Lisa was now more convinced than ever that the situationship with Ken needed to be left alone. It burned too hot and too bright; it needed to simmer. Something more solid needed to boil to the surface because anything that burned that hot would consume everything around it. Lisa was not foolish to think passion alone was sustainable. Perhaps that was why she was so comfortable with Banks, not the combustion-prone Ken. Everything around Ken seemed to catch fire.

Banks was back in Lisa's life. If he was here to stay, then Ken was right: Banks checked all the boxes and there was no point creating unnecessary chaos. She would simply pick things up with Banks.

Lisa dragged her thoughts back to her date with Banks. Last she checked, Ken didn't own IITA. She would not dwell on Ken and his bad behavior anymore.

Coming to IITA was Bank's suggestion, and it had been a welcome suggestion to Lisa because she was hoping they could recreate the magic they once had. Lisa knew Banks hoped the same. Being on a date with Banks meant Lisa couldn't dwell on Ken...or that kiss.

The pair soon lapsed into their old ways and began discussing the Bible. Their conversations were always an intellectual ping-pong centered on two topics: medicine and their faith. They could bounce theories and ideas back and forth all day.

"And what did your friend say?" referring to a Bible passage about the difference between God and humans' measurement of time.

"He said the passage highlights the mercy of God in the eternal nature of God. Since God is eternal and doesn't view time the way we do, He could extend grace and mercy to accommodate repentance."

"Hmm…that makes sense. Because the rest of that passage says something about God's forgiveness, right?" Lisa chimed in.

"Exactly. *He is being patient for your sake. He does not want anyone to be destroyed,*" Banks referred to a Bible passaged. "I never thought of it that way."

"People usually quote that verse to suggest God didn't care how long you've been waiting on Him for something, which is terrifying."

"Exactly! But to see that it's really about an eternal God who uses His timelessness to extend grace and mercy is amazing."

Lisa chuckled at how easily they'd fallen back into this type of discussion. By the time Lisa moved to Ibadan for university, she'd become disillusioned about her Christian faith. Years of playing Ms. Perfect for a church audience had weighed on her. It had always baffled Lisa that church members thought the pastors' calling somehow obligated their children, too. Pastors' children were not allowed to be children. They had to be born perfect and without blemish. She would never forget the day Elder Gbada had a problem with her wearing jeans to church. He'd taught Bible study that morning before church service and used Lisa as an example of how *not* to dress to church. He'd mentioned her by name. Pastor

Chi had been livid. If not for Pastor Dare's diplomacy, the Igbo mom in Pastor Chi wanted to slap the hypocrisy out of Elder Gbada's mouth. Literally.

By the time Lisa moved to Ibadan for her higher education, she'd been ready to get far, far away from any church. And she'd succeeded. Until Banks became her mentor and invited her to fellowship. He'd slowly reawakened a desire to know God, a desire borne out of her own personal conviction, not her parents' or a church audience. Banks had made loving God seem so…normal, like it was the sensible thing to do. So, when they'd started sleeping together, it had been the beginning of the end for them. Banks couldn't get over leading her astray, as he'd said.

"I've missed discussing the Bible with you, Banks. *C'est très bien.*"

"I've missed it, too," Banks responded. "Actually…there's something I've been meaning to talk to you about… I didn't steer us the right way…I let my selfishness get the best of us. And I am sorry for that, Lisa."

"Banks, please don't apologize. I don't blame you for any of it. We were both consenting adults and you never forced me to do anything. If anything, I may have come on strong a few times."

"Me too, Lisa."

"But you should know I am not sorry for being attracted to you. We were in love. You were my first love, and it would have been a problem if there'd been no attraction. The only problem was we didn't handle it the right way."

"*D'accord*. A mistake I don't want to make again, Lisa. I want to get to know you all over again. And I want to do it the right way."

"I'm glad to hear that."

The waiter served them one dessert. Like old times, they'd asked for one piece of cake and two forks.

"Speaking of getting to know you, is this Ken person someone important?" Banks asked between forkfuls of cake.

Banks had heard about the debacle with Adagio, how the strip club had been located near BESEM, to Pastor Dare's vehement protest. After constant faceoff between Pastor Dare and the owner of the Adagio the club had mysteriously burned down in the rain, which led the owner to initiate a lawsuit against the church *and* Pastor Dare for praying to God to send down fire. The owner ultimately lost the case after the court dismissed it, but not before his actions had caused significant headaches for the church community. What Banks had not put together was Lisa's inadvertent involvement with the owner of Adagio, or that Ken was *that* owner. It was time to tell Banks the full story.

"Wow. That is quite a story."

"Yup."

"And are you two still involved?"

"No. Not anymore."

"Looked to me like he isn't happy about that. He would still like to be involved?"

"It doesn't matter. I've made my thoughts on the matter very clear to him."

Lisa decided the kiss she'd shared with Ken was inconsequential. She wasn't being duplicitous, but she also didn't know how to categorize the kiss. The kiss hadn't happened within a relationship; it had been a stolen moment that was now over. She'd not seen or talked to Ken since the kiss. So, there was not much to say there.

"D'accord."

The pair's conversation moved to more comfortable topics. Lisa discussed Ken's mom and Banks gave his opinion. Banks asked Lisa what she'd recently mediated on in her quiet time with God. Lisa said she'd fallen out of practice. Her mornings usually involved rolling out of bed just in time to take a quick shower, pull her hair back in a bun, jump into her scrubs and head out the door as she muttered some impersonal prayer to God. She couldn't remember the last time she took time out for God. Lisa found that sad and promised herself she would change it.

Lisa considered herself Christian. Her faith had been a crutch at best, and a rod at times. She'd used the rod to judge Ken harshly when the real reason why she'd declined Ken's offer – even before the Ije incident – had been because she considered Ken an overcorrection of her mistakes with Banks. Ken was nothing like Banks. She was sure of that, which is why it wouldn't be fair to get involved with Ken because of who he was *not*. Whoever she dated, it would be because of who they were, not who they were not. As Sylvia would say, *'not wanting to be someone is a bad way to live.'* And Lisa agreed. Lisa liked Banks for who he was.

"I want to do this again, Banks."

"Me, too. Lisa. Ibadan to Lagos is not that far. We can alternate trips and talk over the phone. We won't spend most of our time talking about medicine alone. We'll talk about the Bible, too. Focus our attention on things of God."

Lisa nodded in agreement. She looked forward to leaning on Banks as she revitalized her commitment to God.

"And we won't spend so much time alone...isolated from others...behind closed doors. Not a good idea," Banks finished with a wry laugh.

Lisa nodded her head in agreement. What she didn't say was that it wouldn't be hard to do *that* either. Just as the pair parted ways, Banks placed a kiss on her lips and Lisa thought Banks' kiss had been...good

Lisa went back to Mrs. Amadi's room for one last check before heading back to Lagos. Mrs. Amadi was showing improvement. Though hardly perceptible, periorbital edema and facial swelling were improving. Blood that was previously accumulating was now somehow draining. The progress had been confirmed with radiologic examination. Mrs. Amadi's chart acknowledged the slight improvement but hadn't yet attributed it to any treatment plan. Perhaps, the thunderous prayers of Pastor Dare and Pastor Chi struck again. This time, in Ken's favor.

Lisa had been making regular trips to Ibadan to check on Mrs. Amadi, timing them to make sure she didn't run into Ken. If Ken knew she was coming to see his mom, he hadn't let on. And when she couldn't come, Lisa had asked that she be kept in the loop on Mrs. Amadi's progress.

"What are *you* doing here?"

It is said that God hardwired a defense mechanism into all human beings to alert them to the presence of pure evil. The brain sends a signal to hairs on the back of the neck and tells them to be upright standing. Then, a thin, unique chill races down the spine and back up it. At this point, a decision needs to be made - to stay and fight or to get out of Dodge. Well, Dodge wasn't in Lagos, and Lisa wasn't running.

CHAPTER NINE

Dr. Williams' voice is one Lisa could pick out of a cacophony. It was a prickly, nasally combination of sharded glass and nails scratching a dried-up chalkboard. Lisa was sure this was what demons sounded like. A voice that used to intimidate Lisa when she was a medical student until she found her own voice. Certainly not now would she be intimidated. Not *ever* again

"Dr. Williams. Do you need something?" Lisa deliberately sidestepped his question and asked one of her own without turning around to acknowledge him.

"I asked you a question, young lady. Or you don't know how to respect your elders again? You don't have any privileges in this hospital. Or have medical privacy laws and ethics of our profession completely evaporated from that thick skull?"

The demeaning *'young lady'* reference wasn't lost on Lisa. Dr. Williams had refused to acknowledge her certification or refer to her as doctor.

The first time Dr. Williams had propositioned her, Lisa couldn't have been more than sixteen. Dr. Williams had been employed as an internist at UCH at the time and had come into the laboratory where Lisa had been performing some experiments to pick up a lab result. Dr. Williams was the type of person whose skeevy, slimy factor was off the scale; the guy was just a creep. You smelled him before you saw him, and once you saw him, you begged to unsee him. As any female – goodlooking or not – recalls, Dr. Williams had this bothersome intense glare, like a cackle of hyenas sizing up their prey.

Whoever was unlucky enough to be propositioned by Dr. Williams *and* thwarted his advances, may God's mercy be with them because they would need it. What would follow was antagonism at every point. And since Dr. Williams' reach had been far, he did serious damage to the budding careers of many doctors.

What still baffles Lisa is the system that had allowed Dr. Williams to thrive. Many brilliant female doctors had given up and transferred out of the school simply because they could no longer put up with his relentless harassment. Others who stayed built a network amongst each other to warn fellow victims of his presence. Lisa hadn't had many friends due to her age and inability to do what most college students did. Lisa had been in the crosshairs of his wrath for two whole years. Not until Banks got his uncle to intervene had Dr. Williams let up a little.

"As you can see, I am reading a patient's chart. And that is *Dr.* Lisa to you." Still, Lisa did not turn to acknowledge his presence.

"And who do you think you're talking to?"

Lisa thought it best not to engage Dr. William, whom she considered to be a narcissistic bully. Dr. Williams, however, didn't get the memo, as he decided to manually turn Lisa around by her shoulders, which was a mistake Lisa was about to rectify had Ken not chosen that same moment to make his presence known.

"Touch her again, and you die." If Ken's words were not convincing, the darkness that had descended over his countenance like a curtain sure was. Bosco's astride stance and upturned glare weren't messing around either.

Dr. Bayowa who had walked in with Ken quickly deescalated the situation.

"Dr. Williams, you may leave."

"This young lady doesn't – "

"Leave *now*, Dr. Williams," Dr. Bayowa repeated, deciding there and then that it was time to deal with the human stain that was Dr. Williams after all. All the other doctors knew of Dr. William's deplorable treatment of medical residents, especially the female ones. They knew how he made the lives of the female residents who refused his advances unbearable. Why and how they'd tolerated that behavior with their silence was beyond Bayowa. But that ended today. He would personally see to it that dear Dr. William's tenure with UCH ended.

"Just so we're clear," Ken repeated as he stepped in front of an exiting Dr. Williams, "that wasn't an idle threat. If you come near her *again*, I will end your life."

Dr. Bayowa was hardly out of earshot when Lisa's wrath descended on Ken. "I had the situation under control. Threatening to kill someone? Don't you think that's a bit excessive?"

"Given the circumstances?" Ken asked, "It's rather fitting."

"This is what you do now? You just go around beating people up and threatening to kill people?"

Understanding dawned on Ken that Bosco had informed Lisa about what happened with Little Pimp. "I see Bosco is now a snitch." Ken promised himself he'd have a word with Bosco later. "How long has this been going on with that asshole? I never pegged you for a woman who'd let a man put hands on her."

"You have no idea what you're talking about."

"Then tell me. Because if you don't, I'm going to find out and you won't like how I get him to talk."

"You'll beat it out of him? Is this really who you are? I thought I knew you, Ken. Clearly, I had no clue."

"Lisa," Ken said with dead seriousness. "You can marry another man tomorrow and have a thousand children with him. But you must know that there will never come a day when I will stand by idly and watch a man put hands on you."

"I don't need you to fight my battles! I don't need anything from you! I have always been able to protect myself from that...that...that imbecile! And I will do it again! I don't need your methods. How *dare* you insinuate yourself into a matter that doesn't concern you like I am some feckless female?"

Lisa had lost the thin control she had left and was borderline screaming now. It was a miracle that her raised voice didn't wake Mrs. Amadi. Her composure was gone and her left hand was shaking visibly.

"So, this guy has put hands on you before today?" Ken said more to himself than to Lisa. "Well, he's not getting away with it this time," Ken said and would have headed out the door had Lisa not stopped him by blocking his path.

She put her shaking hand on his chest and pushed him back into the room. "You will do nothing! Do you hear me! I forbid you. This is my battle! My fight."

The pair were going back and forth and didn't notice Banks approach them.

"Hey, hey, what's going on?" Banks interjected before he noticed Lisa's shaking hands. Though Banks didn't yet know what had triggered this episode, Banks knew something bad had happened to put Lisa in this state.

"This guy again," Ken muttered to himself before saying to Banks, "Can you see we were having a conversation?"

"Que se passe-t-il?" Banks asked directly to Lisa, his attention fully on her.

"Can you believe this guy, Banks? He just jumped in and started calling the shots like he owns me or something."

"Okay, let's talk about it, Lisa," as he ushered Lisa to a nearby wooden bench in the corridor outside Mrs. Amadi's room and got her a bottle of water.

Banks alternated between holding both of her hands together in her lap and rubbing her shoulders. Only then did Ken notice that Lisa's left hand was shaking and that the shaking was unusual and pronounced. Ken saw that Banks knew what to do, not because Banks was a doctor, but because Banks just knew why Lisa's hand was shaking.

Banks repeated, *"Y'a rien, C'est propre,"* while Lisa had several gulps of water.

"Banks... Dr. Williams was here," Lisa said.

Banks took a moment to take that information in before saying, "The shaky hand makes sense now." Banks was well aware of what Dr. Williams had put young Lisa through while she was in medical school. Though he'd gotten his uncle to intervene and protect Lisa back then, not before Dr. Williams had done damage to Lisa's confidence as a young doctor. It had taken Lisa a long time to rebuild that confidence, and in that time, Banks had learned to let Lisa do it herself. Best to let her ask for help and not force it on her, which is the mistake Ken must have made.

Banks continued, "Ada, you've already won against Williams. You just need to remind that bastard that he can't get to you. And you can do that. You don't have to let him get to you. Just let me know if you need my help in any way."

Ken saw Banks's words blanket Lisa with a calm so surreal, it was difficult for him to believe that only a few minutes ago, Lisa was ready to fight him physically. Ken felt powerless, like he should have known *this* about Lisa; he should have known not to threaten the guy. But then again, Ken would never stand by and do nothing. How was he to know that Lisa would not want him to get involved?

"Ken, I request that you do not contact Dr. Williams in any way at all," Lisa said without looking at him.

Ken did not agree to Lisa's request. He simply walked into his mom's hospital room and left Banks and Lisa in the corridor.

***

She picked up on the second ring.

It had been weeks since Ken's run-in with Lisa, Banks and Dr. Williams at UCH. Ken had thought long and hard about all that happened that day, and one thing had become abundantly clear to him: Banks was a better man for Lisa than he. In the days since, Ken had been trying his hardest to figure out how to let Lisa go. He'd accepted that he should; he simply couldn't, which was why Lisa was the first person he thought to call. He owed her an apology.

"About that Dr. Williams thing, I guess I should have asked... how you wanted to... handle things before riding rough shod over the situation. I'm just not the guy who would react to what I saw any other way. The guy put his hands on you, Lisa. I'm not going to... intellectually process that first. My first thought was to knock his lights out. But..." the next words were hard for Ken to say though he'd been thinking about them for days. "I realize that may not be the kind of guy you want. Banks just *knew* what to do and I...felt...inadequate. I want you to be happy more than anything...more than anything else."

"Ken, I've told you that I don't agree with your views on friendship between a man and a woman. I think we can be great friends. With all the health issues your mom has, I want to be there for you. Friends do that for each other, Ken." There was a pause before Lisa said, "How is your mom doing? Any updates?"

"Fluctuating. She was making some progress the last time I was in Ibadan...when I ran into you. But I was told she had another seizure today," Ken responded. Unbeknownst to Lisa, Ken had heard about every one of her visits to his mom in Ibadan. That Lisa would continue to show so much care for his mom who had never actually met her was incredible to Ken. It proved to him what his heart had first recognized all along: Lisa was a rare gem who cared deeply for people who couldn't care for themselves. That made Ken love her even more. It saddened him that Lisa couldn't see more to him that their past allowed her to see. He wished for another chance to show her he was worth the risk.

"Have you considered flying her out of the country?"

"The first thing I considered. Her doctors – the ones here and the team of doctors they consult with in the States – think she can't fly."

"That makes sense. The altitude may not be the best for cranial pressure."

"Yeah, they said something similar."

"Ken, I'm so sorry your mom is going through this. Let me know if there's anything at all I can do."

"You're doing it, Doc. This is helping. I can't even tell you how much." Ken paused.

Ken still couldn't understand why his mom hadn't told him how sick she was as soon as she'd received the diagnosis. Or better still, once she started getting sick.

"Ken are you still there?" Lisa prompted.

"All this money and there's nothing I can do for her. I can't help her, Lisa. All the money is just useless! Good for nothing. There is no security in money, after all. I can't fly her out. I got the best doctors flown in and they all say the same thing – it doesn't look good."

Ken didn't say anything for a long time, and Lisa listened to the unsaid in his silence.

"Ken, you are doing the best you could possibly do for her. She knows that, Ken. And she is proud of you. Don't worry about what you can't do." Lisa paused before she continued, "It is at points like this – when one runs out of options – that one turns to God. Can I pray with you?"

"Lisa, I have prayed. My mom's prayer group has been praying for her around the clock. It hasn't worked. But maybe God will listen to you. I can see how I'm not His favorite."

Lisa ignored that assumption as she began to pray a simple prayer. She prayed that God would be merciful to Ken's mom and heal her. She prayed that God would give grace to the team of doctors that were treating her. And she prayed for grace for Ken as he went through this journey.

The pair stayed on the phone in silence. Both were lost in different thoughts. Lisa was thinking she would do anything humanly possible to take the source of Ken's pain away. There was no medical intervention she and the brilliant team of doctors at UCH had not floated. Whatever turn Mrs. Amadi was making, good or bad, seemed out of their hands. Lisa didn't want to say it, but Mrs. Amadi was pretty much in hospice care.

"Look, Ken, I've worked with your mom's team of doctors. Resources may be limited here but these guys can go toe-to-toe with any team of doctors in the world. But sometimes…you just get to a point where options are…few…And… as much as I know medical intervention heals, I also know there are cases that are too hard for the practice of medicine. And…it is for those cases…where options are few as they are now…that you pray to a God who heals."

The fear in Ken's silence was loud at the prospect of losing his mom. Ken was scared for the first time in as long as he could remember. Not the fire that burned Adagio had scared him, just like losing his father had not scared him. Asthma, with the damage it did to his family, had never scared Ken. He'd always managed to live a take-life-by-the-horn-and-round-the-rough-corners-hard type of guy. But the idea of being alone scared him. Perhaps he should take Lisa up on being just friends.

CHAPTER TEN

"Bosco, my guy! *How una dey now? I been dey tell you say make you check on me, you no gree. Wetin dey sup now?*"

Bosco was sitting at the bar area of the *suya* spot while Ken worked in the back office. From where he sat, he heard Ije's loud greeting from the entryway of the *suya* spot. *Dis woman again,* Bosco thought to himself.

"*Mba, mba, mba,*" Bosco protested Ije's entry. "Don't come here. You can't come here and be causing trouble. Just turn around and be going."

"*Bosco, me? Now that you and your boss carry go VGC, una no sabi old friends again, abi?*

Ever manipulative, Bosco knew Ije played the guilt card well. But he wasn't falling for it. Bosco had never been able to tell why Ken was chummy with Ije. He'd seen through her from the beginning. She was manipulative and vindictive. Ken had thought Ije was his bridge to the girls that danced at Adagio and hadn't bothered to build a direct relationship with those girls because he'd trusted that Ije was managing them and he -Ken – was managing Ije. What Ken hadn't known that Bosco had known was Ije charged each of the girls a cut of their nightly pay. She'd lorded her closeness with Ken over them heavily.

"Ije, I don't have your time today. And Boss can't see you. Be going," Bosco reiterated.

"Be calming down, I just want to see him on that matter with my crew. He is the one that told us not to come to Black Diamond again. So, *I just want follow am talk about how he fit epp me run some small small business."*

"My boss no dey do your kind business anymore. Ije, come and be going." Bosco was starting to get bothered by Ije's insistence on seeing Ken. There was no way he was going to let her past him into Ken's back office. The last time he let that happen, Ije had slithered her way into Ken and Madam Lisa's relationship and ruined it with her bad vibes. Bosco was determined to never let Ije catch him slipping again.

Just then, Ken came into the bar area from the back office.

"It's fine, Bosco," Ken interrupted the pair. "What do you want," Ken said to Ije.

"*Ehn ehn, fine man. How your body?*" Ije said to Ken with that lascivious look that always bothered Bosco.

"I don't have time. What do you want," Ken repeated to Ije, maintaining physical distance from her.

"*Make we follow talk inside your office now.*"

"No!" Bosco vociferated. "Boss, that is a bad idea. Whatever Ije wants to say, she can say right here."

"I appreciate your concern, Bosco, but I can handle it."

"Boss, *this woman na bad news. The elders for my village talk say -*"

"*Abegi enough with your village people, Bosco!*" Ije interrupted with unusual forcefulness. Then, she quickly recovered with a forced smile and schooled her face with a thinly veiled attempt at pleasantness.

"This way," Ken said as he led the way into his office with Ije on his heels.

As soon as the pair disappeared into Ken's office, Bosco followed them and stood guard in front of the shut door to the back office.

***

Ken heard the tell-tale rhythmic double click and knew what it was before he turned. Ken also knew the only reason why anyone made it a point to cock a gun and then wait to shoot it was to inspire fear. Whatever Ije's reason was for pointing a gun at him, Ken would not give her that satisfaction.

"And here I was, thinking you wanted my help," Ken said with a steady voice that did not betray the panic that was starting to quicken his pulse. "That's a dangerous thing you're pointing at me, Ije. I offered you money-"

"I don't want your money. I had a business that made me my own, but you ruined it," she said with steely calmness. "Would it have killed you to let my people work at Black Diamond?"

"I don't do that type of business anymore."

"Because of *her*?"

"Yes, because of her."

"You think you're better than me now? We were in this business together before she came along. You think she's better than me?"

Not that Ken thought his answer would assuage Ije, but he wanted to keep her talking. Ken didn't believe Ije really wanted to harm him. He also knew that extolling Lisa's virtues to Ije was not the wise move to make.

"You made your point. Now put the gun down and let's talk about what I can do for you."

"I don't want your handouts. I want my business back. The only thing you can do for me is to sign this contract-" she produced a document and placed it on the table in front of Ken while still pointing the gun at him "- and we can be in business."

Ken picked the document up and perused it. The gist of it was that Ije's company would be the exclusive supplier of *waiters* and *waitresses* to Black Diamond in all its locations in perpetuity. The contract was a shell, a front. Of course, these waiters and waitresses would not actually be serving food.

"In what world would I sign this contract?"

"Oh, you will sign it?"

"Or what?" If she was negotiating business with him, then the only purpose of the gun pointed at him was to create duress. Clearly, she needed him alive to do business with "You will shoot me if I don't?"

Ken, ever the daredevil and never known to run from a fight, steadily advanced on Ije until he felt the cold barrel of the gun in Ije's hands on his chest through his white shirt.

***

Bosco was uneasy as he continued to stare at the door. All he heard was silence, which bothered him even more.

"*Dis woman na bad news,*" Bosco said to himself moments before deciding to interrupt whatever was going on behind the door.

***

Ken could see the hesitation in Ije's eyes as he continued their standoff. He was right: she was never going to shoot.

"Is there even a bullet in this thing?" Ken called her bluff on a chuckle, while advancing so that Ije was now the one retreating. Soon, Ije's back was almost at the door.

And that was when Bosco opened the door. The opened door hit Ije and startled her. A loud bang rang out. And then there was silence.

Ken looked at his chest. He looked at Ije with surprised shock. He looked back at his chest to see a red dot on his white shirt at the point where Ije's gun had been. He watched the red dot spread rapidly. Then he felt Bosco's hands around him. He heard Bosco call for help. He heard Ije wail loudly, begging for mercy.

They all sounded so far away.

Ken began to cough even as he felt his chest tighten. He knew he was about to have an asthma attack *with a gunshot wound*, which panicked him. And the more he panicked, the less he was able to breathe. The more he coughed, the harder it was to breathe. Ken smelled the metallic scent of blood with every unsteady breath. Strange as it sounds, he felt fatigue creep into his lungs. They felt sore and heavy inside of him, like they'd been carrying a weight too heavy for them and they were crying for help. For him, it felt like he'd run five kilometers and was catching his breath by breathing through a straw. The more effort he expended trying to fill his spasming lungs, the less air he seemed to actually get, and the sorer they got.

His fingers and toes had begun to tingle. His face, too. It felt like the simultaneous prickly caress of a thousand dressmaker pins. Ken closed his eyes for what seemed like a second. When he opened them back, Bosco was holding him in the backseat of his Bentley while another one of Bosco's boys drove them. Bosco repeated the same command to him, *"Boss, no sleep o! No sleep o! No sleep o!"*

He was gasping now.

He closed his eyes again. When he opened them, they were no longer in his Bentley. Many people were hovering over him while he was laying down on a moving bed. He felt faint. He could hardly breathe at all now.

This is it, Ken thought to himself in silent acceptance. A wry laugh escaped his labored breathing. In that moment, he knew he was dying. So, he thought about Lisa and wondered if she would mourn him. Why would she? He was nothing more to her than some guy that she had a short thing with for a while. Maybe Bosco would miss him. Maybe the people he'd used his money to surround himself with would miss him. But he didn't want to die. He was too young to die. And he wanted to marry Lisa. He wanted to fill his house with kids that looked like him and her, fight with her, make up with her, make love to her.

Darkness appeared, smaller than the size of a pinhead, but quickly grew larger and was fast enveloping light. Flashes of precious memories rushed in and out of his mind. Lucidity ebbed away, one moment at a time. And though his weary body held fast, his life ticked away. There was now more darkness than light. His time had run out.

When one runs out of options, that's when one turns to God. Lisa's words came back to him.

So, he prayed with his dying breath. What did he have to lose?

*Please....,*Ken's internal dying voice said.

In that same moment, an unmistakable Impression settled upon him; the Impression took what seemed like an eternity to unfurl. The Impression pierced through his consciousness and flashed light first, then clarity. With each unfurling layer, the Impression swallowed the darkness that had threatened him only moments ago; and the Impression seemed to say, *"Ask me."*

Ken was sure that what he'd felt like an impression, he'd also heard audibly. He looked at the faces hovering over him, ripping his shirts and putting wires and tubes in him. Though they all seemed blurry and busy, he still couldn't see any proof on their faces that they'd heard what he'd heard.

Ken responded, *What!?*

"Ask. Me," the Impression repeated.

What's he got to lose? He was dying anyway. *Time...more...time.*

"I AM the One who saves. I AM the One who heals.

Swiftly, it was as though a giant palm slapped Ken hard on his chest, causing him to scream in agony.

The slap felt heated as it seared Ken in the place the bullet had pierced through him. The burning touch of the slap felt like it circulated all around his chest cavity first and then travelled throughout his body. Ken gasped even as he felt another slap on his chest. This second slap felt like a command to his mouth to open wide and gulp down life. In compliance, every sac opened up to receive the air that whooshed into them. He felt the giant slap on his chest again. This time, his chest seemed to expand and then sustain in an expanded state. The distention allowed what felt like soothing warm air, unlike the heat of the first slap and the command of the second one, to run through every sac of his right lung first, followed by his left lung. He felt air sacs pop. He felt a simultaneous softening and expansion of the walls of his airways. Then his distended lungs rested, and air rushed out of them through his opened mouth.

Ken inhaled deeply. He let the air out.

And then there was nothing.

CHAPTER ELEVEN

Ken heard Lisa's voice before he opened his eyes.

"He's waking up, Mom."

Pastor Chi and Sylvia were there, too.

"Hallelujah! Hallelujah!" Pastor Chi chanted.

"Where am I?" Ken asked. His voice sounded groggy to his own ears.

"LUTH. You've been asleep for days."

"Hmm…I feel well rested," he attempted humor but saw Lisa was not amused. He could see she'd been crying.

He tried to sit up, but Bosco's hands stopped him.

"Boss, take am easy o," Bosco said.

"I'm fine," he said to Bosco. And to Lisa, he said, "Why have you been crying, Ace?"

Lisa didn't respond to him. She wouldn't look at him. She occupied herself with adjusting and readjusting the pillows behind him.

"I am thirsty. Bosco, can you g-"

"No o! We'll get it," Pastor Chi supplied and beckoned to Lisa. "Let's go and get Kene something to drink."

"I'll stay, Mom. You can just go to the nursing station and ask them."

"Adaolisa, let's go and get Kene water!" Pastor Chi said more forcefully.

"I'm not leaving, Mom."

Ken saw the stubborn pursing of Lisa's lips, which he'd come to recognize as a signal she was immovable on a subject.

"Adaolisa, you've hardly slept a wink for four days. Let's go. We will both come back with food and water for Kene."

"No! I. Am. Not. Leaving."

"Pastor Chi, it's okay," Sylvia said. "Bosco can take us to get the food and water. Lisa will stay with Ken."

Pastor Chi studied her daughter for a few more seconds before giving up and leaving with Syvia and Bosco.

"Ace…"

Ken saw something that threatened his health all over again. Hardly had Pastor Chi left when Lisa began to cry. It started as a soft cry but she soon buried her face in her palms and wept. Lisa was standing by the window; so, he couldn't get to her. He repeatedly beckoned to her to come to him, but she remained where she was and kept on crying. He saw the relief and the fear in the gentle shaking of her shoulders. It was almost too much for Ken to bear. Why he kept being the reason for Lisa's tears, he would never know.

"You scared me."

"I'm sorry," Ken responded.

"You said you would stay away from Ije."

"I'm sorry," Ken responded. "There was nothing going-"

"I don't care about that! You almost *died*."

"I'm sorry," Ken repeated.

"Please don't do that again."

"I won't. I promise. Please come here, Ace. Just come closer and lay next to me."

"I'm fine," Lisa said.

"I'm not. Come lay next to me. Please?"

Lisa slowly made her way to the side of Ken's bed and gingerly settled into Ken's arms. And they both fell asleep.

***

Ken's recovery was rapid. Once the doctors removed the bullet that had narrowly missed vital organs and transfused blood into him, he'd been on the mend. While Ken wanted to visit his mom in Ibadan, the doctors had cautioned him against being in traffic for extended periods of time. He was instructed to avoid anything that could aggravate his breathing or lungs. The doctors had also asked him to prophylactically take routine puffs of his inhaler to ensure he never suffered an asthma attack while his chest was on the mend. At first, Ken thought that was why he'd stopped getting the tightness in his chest that he'd known and lived with almost all his life. But after several weeks had passed and he'd stopped the inhalers, the tightness had not returned. Ken had also noticed that his breathing was easier.

Ken remembered that while the doctors had been working to save his life, he'd felt something in his lungs that had made him breathe deeper than he'd ever breathed even while he was gasping for air. He wondered if his asthma was gone forever but didn't dare to dream. Ken still didn't know what to make of the prayer he'd prayed in those moments and the Impression he'd felt. He was sure he had not hallucinated it. He'd heard the Voice very clearly. He wanted to talk to someone about it and decided the right person was Pastor Chi.

Lisa rarely left Ken's side as he recovered from the gunshot. She'd only leave to go see his mom in Ibadan and bring reports back to him because he'd been unable to travel. Lisa had been with him at all his follow-up appointments, cooked for him and fed him.

Ken wondered if Lisa knew that she was in love with him. He racked his brain repeatedly for any other explanation for why she was so generous with her care towards him and his mom. Was Lisa just a naturally caring person? That could very well be the case; her choice of profession certainly supports that, but it didn't explain the fear he'd seen in her eyes as she watched over him while he was mending. She'd been genuinely afraid he would die; and he'd never seen Lisa be afraid while caring for a patient, not even with his mom. He considered that this was how Lisa cared for those she considered friends, but he didn't think that was it either. Perhaps he was being overly optimistic, but Ken wanted to believe Lisa was in love with him and didn't know it yet or didn't want to face it yet.

Lisa had not made mention of Banks at all, and Ken hadn't asked. Ken was too afraid to hear Lisa say Banks understood that she needed to be by Ken's side during his recovery. Ken just knew the good brother Banks was the type of guy who would be okay with his girlfriend caring for someone she had history with. Unless the tightness of his chest returned and he had reason to refill his vials at LUTH, Ken patiently occupied the friendzone he was back in with Lisa, while he strategized on how to win her over. Good brother Banks was the nice guy; Ken never said he was nice.

***

What is he doing here, Pastor Dare thought to himself as he fellowshipped with the parishioners who stayed back after church service. Some were cleaning, some doing accounting work, and others were huddled together in small groups.

Pastor Dare had just finished his meeting with the church elders. They were still in the process of replacing Elder Gbada. After the melee with Adagio, and the ensuing lawsuit filed against the church by the same person who was gingerly approaching the front pews of the church, Pastor Dare had asked the church Elders to review Elder Gbada's eldership. In Pastor Dare's opinion, Elder Gbada had influenced the Council of Elders to doubt God, and Pastor Dare believed church eldership should grow faith, not doubt. Pastor Dare's proposal for review had met with very little opposition. The Council of Elders had asked Elder Gbada to step down from his eldership, continue to serve in the church, and also informed him that there may be a future chance to reconsider him for eldership.

Though Pastor Dare would have preferred a permanent revocation of Elder Gbada's eldership, he'd reluctantly agreed to the Council of Elders' suggestion without asserting his objections. As it turned out, he'd not needed to assert. Elder Gbada had thought the Council's decision was, to quote him, *"arrant nonsense and a slap on the face of the anointing"* on his head. As such, Elder Gbada had opted to withdraw his and his family's membership from BESEM. Pastor Dare believed some sheep should be allowed to graze other pasture. Last Pastor Dare heard, Elder Gbada was starting his own church.

Pastor Dare continued his conversation with Lawyer Odiase – the same lawyer who'd represented the church in the litigation against Adagio – about a youth program Lawyer Odiase wanted to propose. Since the litigation, Lawyer Odiase had since taken a more active role in church activities, albeit in a capacity he considered more in line with his giftings.

"I think we need to have a robust vocational training program for our youth. If we don't engage them with rigor, the streets will get them, and we don't want that."

Pastor Dare completely agreed with Lawyer Odiase, but he was now distracted by Ken's approach. "Mr. Amadi, I'm afraid you missed the service. We ended the second service a while ago," Pastor Dare directed at Ken.

"And if you wish to resurrect the court case," started Lawyer Odiase, fully in character as the legal representative for the church, "then I must say you're ill-advised, Mr. Amadi. Not only will we-"

"I'm not here for that...or for the service, "Ken interrupted. "I was hoping to talk to your wife – Pastor Chi."

Pastor Dare looked at Ken like he's grown horns. *This guy get chest o.* "My wife. That is not going to happen. What business do you have with my wife?" Pastor Dare responded.

"It's personal. I'd rather not say."

Pastor Chi had reentered the church auditorium from the back office and heard some of the exchange between her husband and Ken. Pastor Chi approached them quickly and said, "Kene is everything okay? How are you feeling? How is your mom doing?"

"I'm much better. She's still the same. Can I talk to you?

"No"

"Yes"

Pastor Dare and Pare Chi said simultaneously before Pastor Chi touched her husband's shoulder to let him know it was fine as she led Ken to the first pews of the church. Pastor Dare and Lawyer Odiase watched the pair like two rottweilers guarding their different agendas. Lawyer Odiase was thinking it was ill-advised for Pastor Chi to have any conversation with a legal adversary without her lawyer present; and Pastor Dare just hated the whole interaction between his wife and Ken. He didn't like it that Pastor Chi had called Ken to pray with him about his mom. *You can pray for her without calling him,* was what he'd told her.

He also didn't like it that Pastor Chi had made several visits to Ken while he recuperated in the hospital. He didn't like it at all. For him, his daughter had the good sense to not date Ken. Ken was no longer in his neighborhood. For all Pastor Dare cared, the matter of Ken was done and dusted. He wished Ken and his mother good health.

Whatever it was Ken came to tell his wife, Pastor Dare couldn't wait to get home and download it from Pastor Chi. Pastor Dare knew it wasn't about Lisa. Lisa had told them she was not involved with Ken or looking to be. Though Pastor Chi may think the two were still *sniffing* around each other, Pastor Dare trusted Lisa's good sense and decision-making abilities.

Maybe Ken was just here to talk about his mom. Maybe he needed counsel or comfort...or prayers. But still, couldn't he go to another church? Why BESEM? *Maybe this is my punishment for not tolerating one problematic sheep*, Pastor Dare thought to himself, referring to Elder Gbada. *Now God is giving me a worse one? God forbid!* It's not like Ken was asking to become a member of BESEM. It would be too awkward for him *and* Ken. But what could Pastor Dare do? He could hardly turn Ken away. Wasn't that kind of his entire job, to seek the lost? What grounds would he have to turn Ken away now without looking like a total hypocrite or *being* one?

"I don't like that your wife is talking to this man *ex parte*, Pastor Dare," said Lawyer Odiase. "You must really caution her against such."

Pastor Dare looked at the person giving him marital advice, his gaze traveling from the unkempt salt-and-pepper afro that seemed sunken in the middle while strangely curved at the edges like Moses had parted the Red Sea on Lawyer Odiase's head, to the well-worn moccasins on Lawyer Odiase's feet, before coming back to rest on Lawyer Odiase's face.

"Lawyer Odiase," Pastor Dare said with contained impatience, "When you marry – and I am praying that *that* will be soon – you will quickly find out that women don't like being *cautioned* or told who they can or cannot talk to. But thank you for the idea about the youth services. I would like to further our discussion on *that*."

CHAPTER TWELVE

Lisa's schedule was slowly normalizing. She still found it hard to believe that Ije had shot Ken, albeit accidentally, according to Bosco's testimony to the police. Ije was currently sitting in jail, awaiting trial; but it was clear to all she would be going to prison for a long time. Gun crimes, even accidental ones, received harsh penalties in Nigeria.

The fear that had coursed through Lisa when she received the call from Bosco that Ken had been shot and was currently unconscious is something she never wanted to feel again. Nothing else had mattered to Lisa as she raced from her clinic to LUTH on a chattered *okada*, altogether forgoing the caution of driving herself, and instead opting to weave dangerously through traffic on the back of a motorcycle. It was not until the *okada* driver said, *"Aunty make una let go small. I get wife for house o,"* did Lisa realize she'd been holding on to the *okada* driver a little too tight and repeatedly muttering, "God, please. God, please." In that moment, as Lisa faced the possibility of never seeing Ken alive again, she accepted that she'd passed the point of no return with her involvement with him. She loved him

In the days and weeks that followed, Lisa had dropped everything else to stay by Ken and care for him as he recuperated. It simply had not occurred to Lisa to leave his side. And when she finally left, it was to do what Ken couldn't do for himself, which was to visit his mom in Ibadan. She made repeated visits to Ibadan and brought reports back to Ken.

Lisa also wanted to tell Mrs. Amadi that her son had been shot by a vindictive and disgruntled past employee. Lisa was convinced that a mother should be informed, at the very least, that her child was in trouble and needed help. It seemed almost unconscionable to keep the information from Mrs. Amadi simply because she was in coma; and the guilt ate away at Lisa with every visit she made to Ibadan. Lisa believed that Mrs. Amadi *could* hear her if she told her that Ken needed her prayers. And so, on one such visit to Ibadan, Lisa whispered into Mrs. Amadi's ears to pray for Ken.

Lisa watched for a reaction from the sleeping Mrs. Amadi but there was none. So, Lisa went back to reading charts.

There was one other business Lisa was resolved to take care of with this visit to Ibadan: it was time to end things with Banks. There was no future for them. And even if Lisa didn't end up with Ken, she still couldn't, in good conscience, continue with Banks, knowing that she could not love him the way she loved Ken. Banks deserved better than that. She would see Banks after finishing up with Mrs. Amadi and let him know her decision.

"You are Lisa."

It can't be. Jarred out of her musings, Lisa knew there were only two people in the room; Lisa was one and an unconscious Mrs. Amadi was the second. Yet, Lisa was certain she'd heard someone speak as she slowly turned around from checking Mrs. Amadi's chart.

Sure enough, she saw the faintly smiling face behind the gentle words she'd just heard looking directly at her. Mrs. Amadi was awake, after being in coma for months. *And she is talking!* Lisa thought to herself. Lisa's years of medical training kicked in and curbed her enthusiasm though she wanted to scream her delight.

"Mrs. Amadi, you're awake. I'm so happy to meet you even if under rather difficult circumstances."

"Why difficult? You want me to die?"

"No, no, no," Lisa hurriedly denied before she saw a very familiar mischievous smirk on Mrs. Amadi's face.

Brain function seems intact. Patient manages humor, a function of the frontal lobe, Lisa thought to herself.

"I am happy to finally meet you. I have heard quite a lot. Let me get the doctor."

"Nonsense," Mrs. Amadi interjected. "*You're* a doctor. Just sit with me for a while."

"I'll call Ken and tell him you're -"

"Why would I want to listen to *that* boy drone on and one about Lisa this, Lisa that, when I can just meet *the* Lisa? Sit with me. It's you I want to talk to."

Lisa didn't quite know what to make of what she was observing. A patient who had been in coma for as long as Mrs. Amadi had been should not be this alert. But Mrs. Amadi exhibited none of those symptoms. Her speech was clear, almost too clear. She seemed content and not at all in a hurry to find out where she was or why she was there. And there was the movement of her eyes: every now and again, Lisa observed that Mrs. Amadi looked past her and smiled in appreciation...*and awe?* Lisa surmised all the monitors attached to Mrs. Amadi would alert her medical team soon enough. Those monitors currently showed stable vitals as Lisa glanced at them.

Lisa furtively pulled a chair and settled it next to Mrs. Amadi's hospital bed.

"You are stunning. Amadi men love beautiful women."

Lisa laughed at the compliment Mrs. Amadi just paid herself. *She is something else,* Lisa thought in admiration.

"And Ken is besotted. He talked on and on about you. He wants to have a large family with you – seven children. I think he missed not having more siblings. I would have loved a big family, but I only have two. And if you think Ken is handsome, you will not believe how beautiful my daughter is."

Lisa watched Mrs. Amadi laugh as she spoke of her daughter in present tense. *That's unusual. Patient exhibits symptoms of memory loss.* Still, Lisa listened. She contributed a laugh here and there as Mrs. Amadi continued her reverie. She wasn't going to tell Mrs. Amadi that her and Ken were no longer together.

"You have someone else?" Mrs. Amadi asked Lisa pointedly and gently.

Lisa didn't want to respond but also didn't want to lie to Mrs. Amadi.

"We were in medical school around the same time."

"Another doctor! Oh dear, he's not the one for you," Mrs. Amadi continued, seemingly oblivious to Lisa's uncomfortable laugh at her presumptuousness. "He will bore you by second year of marriage. A woman like you needs to be kept on her toes. And you and Ken's story already has the makings for that. There's fire, rain, thunder. *Literally*."

Ken's face off with Lisa's dad was funny now but it wasn't at the time.

"My dad did burn Ken's building."

"And if I could choose another father for my son, who better that someone who knows where God keeps thunder?"

At that, Lisa laughed out loud, and Mrs. Amadi joined her. It was like they were old girlfriends, the way they carried on. Mrs. Amadi regaled Lisa with story after story about Ken's childhood. It is true what they say that no one knows a man better than the woman who carried him in her womb. Some of Ken's quirkiness finally made sense to Lisa based on stories his mom told Lisa.

"Mrs. Amadi, I think you should rest now. Let me get your medical staff in here to check you out. It's been such an honor to meet and visit with you, ma."

"Oh dear, I will take you up on that rest. And the pleasure has been mine," Mrs. Amadi responded as Lisa radioed for the nursing station to come in.

"I'm just going to step out to call Ken to let him know you're awake. Ken will be so delighted!"

"You do that, dear."

Mrs. Amadi's medical team of doctors and nurses came in and took over. Lisa quietly relayed some of her observations to Dr. Bayowa as she made her way into the hallway to call Ken and tell him to head down to Ibadan immediately. His mom was awake.

***

For the blessed, living should be loud and dying, quiet. The peaceful passage of one who took life by the horns and held on tight at every eventful turn, every painful heartbreak, should be celebrated. Even angels celebrate the reentry of the valiant.

Mrs. Veronica Amadi stepped out of time and reentered timelessness.

Though Bosco drove as fast as safety considerations would allow him, Ken did not meet his mother awake. He sprinted down the hallway of the most private quarters of UCH, as much as his healing chest would allow, towards his mother's room, not noticing the pitying glances of nurses. He entered her hospital room to find a body covered head to toe with a white sheet, a sight that stopped Ken in his tracks.

The sight before Ken was all too familiar. He'd seen it with his sister, his dad, and now his mom. In that moment, Ken felt utterly alone. With a downturned head and lips, Ken allowed himself to pity himself. A reeling sensation ran through him though he was motionless in the doorway. Perhaps if he never negotiated the distance between where he stood in the doorway and his mother's body, the nightmare before him would go away.

"You just had to hurry back to them and leave me, Mom," Ken said barely above a whisper as he shook his head from left to right while still standing at the doorway. He couldn't go further.

Bosco retreated quietly and called Lisa to come down. He didn't know what else to do.

Lisa's Converse couldn't run fast enough. It was impossible! Only three hours ago she'd carried a *lengthy* conversation with Mrs. Amadi. What is the nonsense Bosco just told her? Lisa cornered hallways like a marathoner, willing her legs to go faster.

"Madam Lisa, be coming o! Be coming now now now. Mama don pass o. Boss no dey alright o."

"No, no, no. I was just there. She's awake."

"She no awake o. Mama don go o. Chai! Na so life be o. Madam Lisa come quick o. Boss no gree move."

"I'm on my way," was the last thing Lisa said before she broke into a run.

Banks had wanted to come with her, but Lisa had declined him, vehemently so. This was not a moment she wanted Banks to be a part of. She needed to get to Ken.

And she came to see Ken still standing in the hallway, frozen in place. The nurses were walking around him as necessary, but no one was bold enough to tell him to move. His face told everyone he didn't want to hear it. He just stood there and watched the comings and goings without so much as a flinch.

Lisa didn't have any words to comfort him with. So, she simply stood beside him.

***

The days that followed Mrs. Amadi's passing were a daze for Ken. The event planner Ken hired to plan his mother's funeral had handled everything when he'd made it clear to her that he wanted something small and solemn with only his mother's close friends and close family. Ken had also wanted to pick out his mother's casket and where it would be interred. Asides from that, he wrote checks and planned to show up for the funeral.

Extended family reached out, some of his mom's old friends had flown in from America to attend the funeral and offer their condolences. It had felt strange receiving their commiseration, especially since it was centered around informing him that she was in a better place. Strange that people still think it was comforting to tell him *that.* If she was in a better place, what good did that do *him*? He wanted to tell them to tell it to her.

This was a road he had to walk alone. When his sister had died, he'd had his mom and dad. When his dad had died, he'd had his mom to grieve with. Now that his mom was gone, he'd have to go it alone. Lisa had called him several times, but he hadn't picked up. Talking with Lisa meant he would risk passing his burdens to her and he didn't want that. She was not his burden bearer.

Pastor Chi had been texting him prayers, Bible verses, and praying hands emojis. Something else Ken had stopped doing was having the periodic check-ins with Pastor Chi who had been teaching him tenets of his new faith, much to Pastor Dare's stern disapproval. Ken hadn't been able to pray or read the Bible either. He woke up, worked out and did physiotherapy, ate hardly, spent a lot of time at work, tried to sleep, and did it all over again. Since he couldn't do what he most wanted to do – which was to be left alone in a dark room all by himself – he did the next best thing: find solace in routine and hope his brain does by rote what his mind found no pleasure in.

Apparently, however, that plan did not sit well with the self-appointed representative of the Nigerian moms association – Pastor Chi. She showed up unannounced at his office in Black Diamond, where Ken had been holed up for days, demanding to see him. What surprised Ken more than Pastor Chi driving to VGC to Black Diamond, was that Pastor Chi also brought food for him - *Ofe nsala* and *fufu*.

"This is a restaurant, Pastor Chi. There's food here," Ken tried impatiently.

"My friend, eat," Pastor Chi hissed.

"Do you intend to stand over me and watch me eat?"

"Yes," she responded curtly. "And it is time to leave the beard gang. Are you trying to look like the devil? Enough of it already."

Ken remembered he'd consumed a lot of coffee in the last few days, but he couldn't remember tasting anything else that he'd put in his mouth. The bittersweetness of the *nsala* worked its magic to awaken Ken's appetite. Also, the sooner he ate, the sooner Pastor Chi could leave. The sooner he could go back to being alone in his office.

"I know you're grieving," Pastor Chi said in a kinder tone, "but you need food to grieve, okay! I am going to send food again tomorrow. I already gave Bosco my number and I've told him he should call me if -"

"Pastor Chi, you can't be ordering my st-" Ken interrupted.

"Kene, don't interrupt me," was Pastor Chi's stern retort. "I've told Bosco to let me know if you don't eat your food. Do you want me to come back here *everyday*, and watch you eat?"

"I'd rather you didn't."

"Then eat the food I send." With that, Pastor Chi left.

Lisa got double dose of stubbornness, Ken thought to himself. Lisa….Ken wanted to talk to her, to lean on her. Ken ran his tired hands over his face and through his beard. Pastor Chi was right; it was time for the beard to go.

***

Grieving is a long and personal process. It can be dark and lonely. Inevitably, however, light will beckon; and the grief-stricken will have the chance to embrace the comfort of light.

For Ken, the light was his work. Over the next few weeks, Ken worked like a mad man because he needed a project to pour all his energy into. Some investors had inquired about franchising opportunities for Black Diamond in other big cities. Even Abuja came calling since Black Diamond was conservative enough. So, he began to work on developing a franchise business model. He convinced one of his college friends who'd flown in from the States to attend his mom's funeral to relocate and help him. His friend – Agyei – is a Ghanaian graduate of Havard Business School. Living in Nigeria meant Agyei could see his family in Ghana more often. So, relocation sat well with him.

The pair went to work as days turned into weeks. During one of their informal business meetings at Ken's VGC home, Agyei suggested next steps for franchising Black Diamond.

"Why don't you test it out with the Adagio lot?" Agyei suggested. "Brand recognition is key to successful franchising. The Adagio lot is prime real estate and offers a great opportunity to build the first Black Diamond franchise. The story of that building will sell it with little effort!"

"No," Ken stated "I don't want Black Diamond to have any other location in Lagos. Each State in Nigeria only gets one Black Diamond."

"That limits market penetration. Don't forget the multi-million-naira monthly subscription," Agyei countered.

"I don't want to penetrate the market. The brand is opulence and exclusivity. Market penetration is not my agenda for Black Diamond"

"And the price point?" Agyei asked.

"Value," Ken supplied. "They know the value that comes with being in a place like Black Diamond."

"To drink expensive liquor and relax? They can do that in their front porch."

Agyei, like many others Ken had discussed the Black Diamond business model with, didn't get it. Monthly subscription for a club membership was not a new thing; country clubs have been doing it for decades.

Ken never defended his actions in business, but his business partner was a different matter.

"Have you heard about the merger between Tade's company and Appdt?"

"Of course: an IT firm buying the leading Nigerian collective of freelance app developers. But what has that got to do with Black Diamond," Agyei questioned.

"Everything," Ken responded. "The discussion that led to that merger was initiated over pours of Macallan. I introduced them. All the stuff everyone saw on television was just fluff. A multi-million-naira monthly subscription is *nothing* compared to the value we deliver. It doesn't even gate-keep. The people we turn down would gladly pay double that to gain access. Black Diamond is where deals that will change the economic landscape of Nigeria will happen. Maybe all of Africa."

"I see," understanding dawning on Agyei.

"Do you? Cause I need your buy-in if we're going to roll together on this."

Just then, Lisa's call came through.

Ken ignored it.

"You're still not taking her calls. Bruh, the only help I can offer you is to go out drinking, but I know you don't drink. Maybe you should connect with this girl."

"I'm making moves but she's still with that guy."

"So?"

"She's not that type of girl."

"Ken, if you think she's *the* girl, the more reason to fight for her and let the better man win."

Ken let out a deep sigh. He wasn't sure if he was the better man for Lisa. Since Lisa discovered he was the owner of Adagio, Ken couldn't remember a time when any of their interaction had been pleasant for her. If he wasn't botching the stuff with Dr. Williams, he needed comfort. It pained him to burden Lisa. However, if Ken had been a better man, he would have left her alone with what's-his-face; but Ken wasn't, especially not when he was sure Lisa was in love with him.

"These things take time," Ken said cryptically before routing their conversation back to business. "I do have an idea for the Adagio building. I think that location – which is already next to the church – would be great for church business. God already took an…interest in it," Ken chuckled mirthlessly.

"Ken, that location is prime real estate. That church cannot afford it."

"I know. Which is why I am giving it for free," Ken said to the consternation of his friend and business partner.

"And the middlemen strike again! Bruh, Nigerian pastors are a different cut."

"The middlemen?" Ken asked.

"The self-appointed mediators between God and man. These pastors and their fleecing of their congregation. They got you, too! Ken, that is prime real estate. You can't give it away. That's bad for business."

"First of all, Pastor Dare didn't ask me and doesn't know anything about my intentions yet. Knowing him, he will probably decline my offer. And not everything is about business, Agyei. Money is not everything; trust me on that."

"Listen, I may not be big balling like you, but I was doing very well in the States. If I am going to relocate here to join you in business, I need to know that you've not become some religious zealot who is going to be making unsound business decisions"

Ken considered what Agyei said. Him, a zealot. Now, that was funny.

"Noted," Ken responded. "But you should know that I *am* going to give the Adagio lot to the church free of charge. And if you're opposed to that, I'm afraid we are at an impasse. You should also know that things are going to be different from the way we rolled back in the States. I know we made a lot of money doing different types of businesses, but I am fully committed to finding better ways to make even more money. And if you are not cool with that, let me know now. I will pay you well for your troubles and send you on your way."

The two men faced each other down before Agyei said, "She's *that* fine? Cause this ain't Jesus."

Ken laughed before saying, "It's Jesus...but she is fine."

CHAPTER THIRTEEN

It has been a few months since Mrs. Amadi's passing. In that time, Ken had not made one attempt to contact Lisa in any way. She'd tried seeing him at the *suya* spot but he was never there. She even visited Black Diamond to no avail. Black Diamond, Lisa thought, was poised to be a tremendous success in Lagos. It was already the talk of several gossip blogs and considered the stamp of approval that one was finally rich and relevant in this Lagos. Anyone who thought themselves rich but couldn't get into Black Diamond hadn't quite arrived in the upper echelons of Lagos. From what Lisa gathered, Black Diamond had a rigorous vetting process for membership. So, wealth alone was not the criterion for membership.

From its location in Victoria Garden City right by the beach, to the exquisitely dressed staffers, everything dripped premium. There was only one doorway into the establishment, and that doorway faced the ocean on the other side of the entry gate.

This design was to ensure exclusivity and to keep the prying eyes or phone cameras of uninvited guest out. Black Diamond was considered a playground sans drama for the ultra-rich, ultra-influential.

All she'd heard about Ken recently was through her mom. Pastor Chi was still in almost-daily communication with Ken, to the dismay and disapproval of Lisa's Dad. Lisa knew Pastor Dare *knew* when his wife could not be dissuaded; and when Pastor Chi was dealing with a lost sheep, which is what she thought she was doing with Ken, there was no dissuading her. So, Pastor Dare simply watched his wife cater to his...nemesis. Pastor Chi was the one who told Lisa that Ken had started visiting church and started meeting with her to study the Bible. Pastor Chi was also the one who told Lisa that Ken had somehow been miraculously healed, which is why he'd not had the need to visit LUTH anymore.

Lisa ached to hear all of this from Ken...but it seemed he'd shut her out. He was finally letting go, she thought. Perhaps Ken was staying away because of Banks. While Lisa had ended things with Banks, Ken was not yet aware. Also, the Ken she knew would not back off because of Banks. It must be that he'd finally let go. It was what Lisa had asked him to do. Still, it hurt.

She'd tried calling him to no avail. He wasn't picking up her calls. More than anything, Lisa just wanted to see how he was doing with her own eyes. And since she wasn't sure he would let her in if she showed up at his office or home, she opted for a far-fetched option: she would go to her parent's house and hope Ken would visit Pastor Chi.

***

"You both got off on the wrong foot."

"Ha! Wrong foot *kwa*! Mummy please, *you dey whine me*. Daddy *thunderized* his building. We all saw it with our naked eyes!"

"Don't you have some sons of Babylon to go and meet?" Pastor Chi asked rhetorically.

"Mommy, mommy, mommy, nobody calls them *sons of Babylon* anymore. They are sons of b-"

"Son!" Pastor Dare hurriedly interrupted. "Come and be going. Thank you o!"

"Okay o. Ken-ken, I hail you o. *We go dey yarn later abi*?"

"Sure," Ken responded, amused by the family dynamics. Emeka was so vastly different from Lisa.

He was also surprised by how patient Pastor Dare was with Emeka. The whole bit was odd to Ken.

"As I was saying, you've both butted heads over very personal matters."

"I disagree with you, Chiamaka." Pastor Dare interrupted his wife.

Pastor Chi had felt it necessary to broker peace between the two men, although it was clear to Ken that Pastor Dare didn't want this meeting.

"While I commiserate with Mr. Amadi on the passing of his mother, I think our business is concluded. If only he would stop showing up at my church, all will be well. If you ask me, it seems Mr. Amadi keeps prolonging what is otherwise sufficiently concluded."

"Ken is a Christian now," Pastor Chi supplied.

"And I am happy for him. Sincerely!"

"I'm also a member of your church," Ken chimed him.

"That is not an option. I don't have any vacancies in my membership roster this year. Check back next year."

"Fine. Pastor Chi is my pastor," Ken retorted as the two men continued their you-can't-be-my-friend face off.

"No, she cannot! You cannot go from sniffing around my daughter to sniffing around my wife!"

Ken laughed at that. "You think I'm *sniffing* around Pastor Chi. I am charming but I am not that charming. I don't have any designs on your wife, Pastor."

"I didn't mean *that*. You are right that you're not that charming. But you can't pursue any kind of relationship with my wife, not even a pastor-parishioner one. She can't be your replacement..." Pastor Dare caught himself before saying what he was about to say, which would have been unkind.

"Mother? You think I want your wife to be my mom?" Ken paused before continuing, "I want to know more about God and Pastor Chi is teaching me. That is all. As for the business that brought us together, I have found conclusion that you might find acceptable. I would like to give the Adagio lot and all the surrounding land I have since purchased to the church. My understanding is that the church is looking to build a campus of some sort. This should help. I am also willing to support the building of the campus financially."

Ken paused to let Pastor Dare get a word in, but it seemed none was forthcoming. Pastor Dare had a quizzical look on his face.

Unbeknownst to Ken, Pastor Dare was recalling his conversation with Filomena. He'd prayed to build a home where people like Filomena could live rent-free while they got back on their feet. The home would be more like a hostel and would include a hall for vocational training, a small farm where the young women could grow simple fruits and vegetables and maybe a daycare for the ones who had little ones. *Lost sheep need actual food, not only the Word,* had been Pastor Dare's thought. He'd thought to himself that Filomena needed to be guided and helped in her commitment to turn her life around and feeding her the bread of the Word of God was not enough. She also needed social services. Pastor Dare had not mentioned that to anyone, not even to Pastor Chi. Yet, Ken was now telling him that the same building that had caused Filomena to turn her life around was being donated to BESEM to use to help Filomena.

"You won't have to do anything except accept the building."

"Don't you want to get paid for it? You *are* a businessman, after all," Pastor Dare threw Ken's words back at him.

"I don't want payment. This is going to be a gift to the church."

"Why?"

"Because I want to," Ken stated matter-of-factly.

"Just like that?"

"Should there be more to it?"

"That's a lot of money you'll be giving away."

"At the risk of confirming your opinion of me and stating the obvious, I am a very wealthy man. Holding on to that building was never about money."

"It was about principle. You wanted to keep it in my face. To remind me that you are still in my face."

Ken did not need to answer. Pastor Dare's estimation was on the money.

"Still," Pastor Dare continued, "I thank you on behalf of BESEM for the gesture, for thinking of serving this community that way. However, I do not think you should be parting with such a sizeable gift while you are…grieving. But I will pray on it and discuss with the church elders."

"I am of sound mind, if that's what you're worried about. You should know that I am already decided on this," Ken replied. He also heard what Pastor Dare was not saying. This building, after all, is at the root of the discord between the two men.

"And I can see that, but I have to do what is right here, no matter what. I do not think it is okay for you to make such a decision while you are grieving the loss of your mother. The gift may not be sizeable to you, but it *is* sizeable. Before BESEM can accept it, I must make sure it is right to do so."

From where Ken was seated, he could see Pastor Dare was genuinely not considering the gesture as a victorious conclusion to the matter that started it all. The average person would jump up and down and be excited to take possession of the building, seeing as Pastor Dare told him severally to take the business of Adagio elsewhere. Yet, here the two men were, and Pastor Dare was hesitating, and his hesitation was because he wanted to make sure accepting Ken's gift was the right thing to do. Ken found this highly commendable.

Ken was not worried at Pastor Dare's hesitation. He was confident this was the right conclusion for the Adagio building; and the right thing would sort itself out eventually. For a moment, it seemed the men had arrived at a coinciding confluence. Until the conversation pivoted to the matter of Lisa.

"There is another matter I would like to discuss with you. I want to marry Lisa, and I would very much like your blessings." Ken said without much preamble. He continued by informing Pastor Dare that he was a changed man and his love for Lisa had grown. Ken shared that though he'd not been in contact with Lisa since his mother passed, he'd taken the time to allow Lisa to clarify her feelings for him and sort out her relationship with Banks, and that he fully intended to resume his pursuit of Lisa.

***

Fewer things irked Pastor Dare more than people who thought knowledge or means somehow replaced experience. If anything, *that* mindset was itself revealing of the knowledge deficit of such people. In Pastor Dare's experience, there was no other area where people thought they were wiser than experience than in the area of love and relationships.

Currently sitting on the settee across from Pastor Dare was Ken. The reversed position was not lost on Pastor Dare. It seemed he was ever on opposite ends with this particular young man who was currently extolling the virtues of being in love with Lisa.

Pastor Dare silently observed Ken who appeared overly confident with his head cocked to one side and very minimal hand gestures. All traces of cautious movement from his gunshot wound gone, Ken owned his space on the sofa. It was obvious this young man had practiced his presence, which made Pastor Dare smile. So much effort put into image.

As Ken spoke, Pastor Dare only caught every few words because his attention was more focused on observing the young man himself. Ken carried on about Lisa and his intentions to marry her.

"Why are you seeking my permission now? You didn't need it before," Pastor Dare asked.

"It's the right thing to do," Ken responded.

"I see," Pastor Dare responded, although he really didn't. The young man said he'd become a Christian because he'd had some encounter with God. What Pastor Dare failed to understand was why Ken thought the first order of business was to seek permission to court Adaolisa even though the same Ken was aware that Adaolisa was involved with someone else. Now, Banks was a fine young man who Pastor Dare was hoping would marry Lisa. Of course, it was ultimately up to Lisa.

"I love her more than I can put into words. And I want to marry her. I will take care of her and - "

"You've said that three times now, that you love her," Pastor Dare interrupted. "Like it's supposed to mean something to me."

"I should hope so. I should hope you want your daughter to marry a man who loves her."

"Of course, I do," Pastor Dare surprisingly agreed. "But I don't think you love her or know what love is."

Pastor Dare could see from Ken's expression that the young man felt taken aback, maybe even insulted.

"I don't know what love is," Ken repeated.

"No."

"And I'm guessing that's because I'm not a veteran Christian like you?"

"No, it's mostly because you're young. It's also because of the type of man I know you to be."

Ken began to chuckle, and Pastor Dare let him and watched him. He waited for Ken to share his mirth, while having a smirk on his own face.

"Pastor, you don't know me."

"I know enough. You're the young man who is trying to interlope Lisa and Bankole's relationship. I'm guessing that's because you don't care that she's dating someone else. You just want what you want. You are the young man who makes money by delivering *pleasures* to people. You employ women and ask them to take their clothes off to entertain other people. And I can bet that you think your line of work is fully justified."

"Lisa is available to be pursued until she is married. So, you are right; it doesn't really matter to me that she's involved with Banks. I don't own any other strip clubs, and I don't plan to. And…um…justified or not, I'm not answerable to you on that."

"That may be right. Yet, here you are in *my* living room, asking for *my* blessing to court my daughter. And I cannot give it to you, knowing what I know."

Again, Ken began to chuckle. Pastor Dare could see he wasn't as unbothered as he was a few moments ago.

Pastor Dare was in unfamiliar territory here. Unlike the last time he sat across from Ken like this to negotiate– and Pastor Dare very much felt that this, too, was a negotiation, - he wasn't fully sure God sanctioned his current position. That was shaky grounds for Pastor Dare. There was the dream his wife had had; Pastor Chi's dreams were always shockingly accurate. In fact, he'd come to think of Pastor's Chi's dreams as snapshots of a future event. He believed Pastor Chi got these microcosmic glimpses of the future. Not one of her dreams as ever not actualized.

And apart from the dream, Pastor Dare had also been praying for God to remove Ken from Lisa's life completely. It has been a divine radio silence on the matter. Instead, opportunities for Lisa to be further involved in Ken's life had come up. His experience in walking with God has thought Pastor Dare that God didn't discuss settled matters. Still, Pastor Dare held on to the possibility of God settling the matter in *his* favor, which would mean Ken would vamoose like a fart from his daughter's life.

Pastor Dare rearranged himself on his and Pastor Chi's love seat and continued, "Love is not a feeling," he began.

"Is that right," Ken offered noncommittally, reigning his anger in at what he considered condescension.

Pastor Dare tried again.

"My mother-in-law was much older than her husband, Pastor Chi's father. Their first child, my brother-in-law, lives in Kano. *He* is much older than Pastor Chi. He was conceived when Pastor Chi's mother was rather young. She wasn't...shall we say...born into a religious home; and she...wasn't... discreet. So, she had her son...didn't know who the father was. *Her* parents – Pastor Chi's grandparents – threw her out of their house. This seventeen-year-old young girl took her child and set out into the world on her own, and it was rough for her. Somehow, she turned her life around. Got a steady job and was living a modest life with her son. She joined my parents' church. She gave mercy that wasn't given to her. She had this unique way of reaching young people and the right words to help them turn their life around."

Pastor Dare paused before continued. He hoped Ken understood the importance of the story he was sharing with him. Though Pastor Dare had abridged it, this was a story that was so dear to him, one that probably laid the foundation of his marriage to Pastor Chi.

"But she was unmarried until she was forty. Unfortunately, the supposed stigma of being a single mom is one that even the church of Christ still can't figure out how to deal with. No single brother asked about her; no one was interested. Not until Pastor Chi's father, who was over ten years younger than my mother-in-law, showed up. Without wavering or any equivocation, he pursued her and married her, despite wagging tongues and the disapproval of his parents. And their union was blessed with another child – Pastor Chi. He fathered his wife's older son with the same devotion and the same love he did his own blood child."

"Here is my point," Pastor Dare continued, "*that* is what I married into. I married into a legacy of unconditional love that defies stigma and odds."

Pastor Dare rose to his full height. He paced for a bit before he came to stand in front of his guest. "So, when I say you can't have my daughter, it is because I don't see in you a man who can love her despite all odds. Can you love her beyond your boundaries? Do you even know what that means? I just don't see you – a man who serves pleasure – as that type of man."

Ken stood up. In doing so, Pastor Dare realized this was the closest he'd ever been to Ken. He watched Ken head towards the door before he paused and turned around to say, "I am going to marry Lisa. I am going to defy whatever stigma you think *I* carry. I am going to overwhelm your odds. And I am going to extend that legacy you spoke of."

Just as Ken was about to exit the living room, as his hands circled the doorknob, Ken paused again and turned around. He seemed to deliberately take in Pastor Dare's living room for the first time that evening. With a smile on his face, Ken said, "So, this is where Lisa grew up...hmmm." Then he turned around and left.

Pastor Dare continued to watch his closed front door quizzically.

Unbeknownst to both men, Lisa had heard it all. She'd made a visit to her parents after her workday and fallen asleep in their room. She'd woken from her nap to muffled voices she'd soon recognize as Ken's and her dad's. Her intention was to join the men, since she'd visited her parents' in hopes of running into Ken. While Ken's relationship with her mom continued to blossom, she couldn't imagine why her dad would want to visit with Ken. Upon hearing the men's conversation, she'd opted to hide her presence and simply listen.

Lisa was not happy at what she'd heard her dad say to Ken. And she was poised to tell him as much the moment she made her presence known after Ken's departure.

Pastor Dare was still staring at his closed front door when Lisa said, "Do you think you are better than Ken?"

Pastor Dare turned around to where his daughter was standing, looking at him with...reserved disappointment on her face?

"Do you think you're more righteous than Ken?" she repeated.

Pastor Dare didn't answer. He was still discerning the disappointed look on her face. Adaolisa had never looked at him like that. She seemed so sad.

"The problem I have with people like us is that we can't see that we are who we are only by the grace of God. If the same pain, loss, and grief that touched Ken and his family touched you, Dad, you have no idea what or where you would be. All you've known is the goodness of God; it is so common to you that you think everyone else has the same experience. You were raised by loving parents who literally adored the ground you walked on. No trauma, no pain touched your childhood. And you married the love of your life whom you met rather early in life. And she, too, adores the ground you walk on. You've known nothing but God's goodness. And I know it's easier for you to show grace and mercy when it is not personal, but when someone needing grace shows up to your front door, when it is in your backyard, that's a different story. And I just don't think that's what Jesus would do."

And with that, Adaolisa, too, walked out.

***

"Chiamaka, do you think I'm judgmental?"

"Before *nko*? We are Nigerian parents. If we don't judge, *wetin we for do?*" Pastor Chi finished on a laugh before she realized her husband wasn't sharing her humor.

"Chi, Adaolisa said something to me today…I don't know what to make of it."

"Is it only Adaolisa that said something to you?"

It would appear that Ken had called Pastor Chi to brief her on the two men's conversation.

"He told you already?!"

"Yes, he called me," Pastor Chi nodded her agreement.

"Aaargh! I don't like that man," Pastor Dare exasperated, getting up from his repose on the bed. He paced over to the vanity. "And I don't like that he keeps calling my wife behind my back! This is not the way to get what he wants, Chiamaka."

"Dare, calm down. He is not sniffing around your wife," Pastor Chi was amused by her husband's jealousy and possessiveness only when it came to Ken. Poor man thought Ken was trespassing into all he held dear. And it seemed the women in his life were cooperating with the enemy at every turn.

"But why must he call you so much. He is so needy! And why do you keep talking to him, Chiamaka?"

"He is a new Christian and he needs guidance. I am not going to turn my back on him to assuage your," Pastor Chi started to laugh uncontrollably while saying, "fears *and* possessiveness. Kene does not want your women...well, he wants one."

Pastor Dare whipped around to see his wife bawled over laughing at his discomfort. "Chiamaka, stop laughing."

"Okay. Sorry." She stood to calm her pacing husband and asked, "What is the worst that could happen?" This was something the pair did when a matter seemed overwhelming to them; it was their way of deflating any problem that seemed too big. Pastor Chi gave it a try here although she wasn't too sure *this* was the type of problem one could deflate. From Pastor Dare's vantage point, the future of their daughter was at stake with a man whom he was convinced couldn't be a good husband despite his best intentions.

Pastor Chi agreed. But Pastor Chi also knew when to stop fighting. This was a matter that was decided. What she'd not told Pastor Dare was that she'd had a repeat of the same dream: She and her husband walking to church with their twin grandchildren. They were bookending their grandson and swinging his arms on either end. Ken and Lisa were walking behind them. Only in this second dream, Ken was holding Pastor Dare's Bible while holding a little girl with his other arm.

Pastor Chi knew one thing as sure as she knew her own name: if she dreamt a dream twice, it would happen exactly as she dreamt it; it was only a matter of time. So, she stopped fighting the inevitable and began praying for grace. The way Pastor Chi saw it, if Adaolisa was going to marry Ken, then she welcomed the opportunity to disciple Ken into a good Christian man with glee.

"Dare, what is the worst that could happen if Adaolisa marries Kene?" Pastor Chi repeated.

With obvious hesitation, Pastor Dare said, "He hurts her and leaves her…with kids she has to raise alone"

"No, that's not the worst. You're telling me if Lisa shows up to our house with her children and says her husband left her, won't we take her back and step in?"

"We will," Pastor Dare agreed.

"Then that's not the worst." Pastor Chi moved closer to her husband and placed her hands on his shoulders. "The worst that could happen is we are not there to catch her fall." She watched on Pastor Dare's face as that realization sank in. And she saw his fear, the same fear that would have been mirrored in her own eyes had she not assuaged them with heavy prayers.

"And if that happens," Pastor Chi continued, "what do you think happens *then*?"

Pastor Chi saw her husband fight back tears as he quietly answered, "Adaolisa will get herself back up and move on."

"Yes," Pastor Chiamaka nodded her agreement. "She will get herself back up and move on. Because that is the woman we raised," she finished with a shrug. "We put all we can in these children; we commit them into God's hands and then we trust that what we've put in them is enough. Dare, we can't force her in one direction or the other. I have heard you provide the same counsel to other parents."

"My daughter is different."

"I know. Your *precious* Adaolisa."

Between the possessiveness and his obvious frustration, Pastor Chi had never seen her husband this troubled. And the only reason her Dare would ever be this troubled is because he wasn't sure God was on his side.

"Do you know what he said to me? Your *precious* Kene," which would be the first time Pastor Dare had called Ken's name. "He said he will extend *my* legacy. He didn't say it like a threat, either. He said it like….a church announcement. Like…"

"He was sure of the outcome," Pastor Chi offered.

"Yes! Exactly! He said it like he was sure there was no other outcome. Does he know something I don't know?" A thought occurred to Pastor Dare, but he was too troubled to even voice it. "Is Adaolisa pregnant?"

"No, she's not.

Pastor Chi smiled to herself. She now knew more about Ken than her husband did, and she knew that if it had to do with Ken's convictions, no one could stop him. Pastor Chi often prayed that more Christians would have the same convictions about their faith and walk with God that Ken had about business and his devotion to Adaolisa. Pastor Chi also thought Ken's conviction was reminiscent of another man she knew, the same man standing in front of her right now. The man who usually stands tall and firm in his faith in God, yet currently pacing with unsure steps, and seeking a way out of what he perceived to be a conundrum.

"Maybe you should put your reservations aside for a moment and really get to know Kene, Dare," she said to her chagrined husband. "What you find out may surprise you."

CHAPTER FOURTEEN

Following all Lisa heard during Ken's visit with her dad, Lisa decided to pay Ken a surprise visit at his VGC mansion with a bit of trepidation. The last time she'd paid Ken a surprise visit at Adagio had not ended well. She'd ended up being surprised to find Ije's head in Ken's lap. The memory of that event hadn't faded much. She'd declined several attempts by Ken to discuss it. That was Lisa's way of dealing with something that was in the past and was too painful: she moved on and never talked about it again. She realized that method may have helped her for some things, but relationships were a different matter. She just didn't know how to tell Ken how she felt about what she'd seen that day. She could never find the words to say it was common sense that someone who cheated once will likely cheat again; so, her inability to simply walk away from Ken made her feel weak. And she hated being weak.

Yet here she was at Ken's front door, hoping to see that he was well, and wanting to care for him if he wasn't. Whether this was weakness or strength, time would tell.

"Hello, Lisa," Ken said to Lisa's sigh of relief.

"How have you been?"

"I'm good. Hey, thanks for everything, Lisa. I really appreciate it. I take it Bosco is how you found my home. Not that I mind. I'm glad you're here. I wasn't ghosting you or anything. I just needed some things to sort themselves out...," Ken's voice trailed off.

Lisa went to sit beside Ken on the floor next to the wall that bordered the stairwell, Ken's favorite place in this whole mansion. Ken was eating some of the food that Pastor Chi had sent by courier earlier in the day.

"You don't have anything to apologize for," Lisa hurriedly discouraged Ken's apologies. She didn't quite know what to say or why she was here. She was simply glad to see he was doing well. "You're not alone, Ken. I just want you to know I'm here for you," was all Lisa could manage."

"Thanks," Ken responded.

"And you've struck a good relationship with my mom, which I still can't believe."

"And I'm sure your dad would gladly skewer me for that."

"He'll come around. Dad has not met a lost sheep he didn't want to save."

"Really? I don't get that from him. I think he would gladly roast *this* sheep. According to him, I keep *sniffing* around his women."

The pair laughed dryly. He now attended BESEM regularly. Since he donated the vacant lot that used to be Adagio – which Pastor Dare had reluctantly agreed to after the council of elders jubilantly accepted Ken's gift – Ken's membership in BESEM had been welcomed by all parishioners. Ken had also donated a very hefty sum to start construction of the hostel and services center to help reintegrate displaced people back into society. He'd also inadvertently supplied the name the establishment would be called: House of Merciful Embrace – HOME. He'd since gone from villain-worthy-of-God's thunder to hero to the entire BESEM church community. He regularly visited Pastor Dare's vicarage to meet with Pastor Chi. He'd even achieved the drop-by-unannounced status with Pastor Chi. But Pastor Dare had only slightly thawed and not fully warmed up towards him yet. Ken was now the happy recipients of Pastor Dare's up-nods; going from 'Mr. Amadi' to 'Mr. Kene." Ken considered this a positive change in the relationship between himself and the man whom he was certain would be his father-in-law.

"It's still so easy to talk to you, Ace. I'd suffer a lifetime of asthma if there was a chance it would intersect our paths. I would gladly be shot all over again, too."

"I don't find that funny at all, Ken. And you've not been doing much of that lately...talking to me," Lisa said with uncharacteristic vulnerability.

"I'm sorry about that, Lisa. Out of respect for you, I was hoping you'd take that time to sort out your current relationship. I was also using that time to learn more about Christianity."

"I heard. Pastor Chi told me. She said you somehow don't have asthma anymore?"

"It seems that way. I haven't felt any of the symptoms since the shooting. I really thought I would die that day. Then I remembered what you said, that I should pray when I don't have any other options. Again, I was faced with the limitations of money and success. They're good to have, don't me wrong, but.... the Guy upstairs is the wealthy One. Cause He trades in time; and as a businessman, I know time is the scarcest resource on this Earth. You can't buy it anywhere. Mine ran out that day, and He put some more time on my clock...like it was nothing to Him. Can't beat that with a baseball bat."

Lisa smiled at Ken's version of a testimony. Only Ken could tell *it* like that.

"How is Brother Benson?"

Lisa laughed at the petty diss. "You know his name is not *Benson*."

"Oh, my bad," came Ken's fake apology. "I'm sure it'll come to me."

Lisa hadn't told Ken she and Banks were no longer together. The progression she'd been hoping for had never happened. While the lackluster kiss they'd shared at IITA had not helped matters - Lisa thought it had felt like chewing dry *garri* – Lisa's acceptance that she was irrevocably in love with another man had nailed the coffin on her relationship with Banks. Also, Banks still harbored global aspirations; and Lisa could not keep him from doing something that was so needed in the world. May a better woman than her find brother Banks.

She was looking at the man she never wanted any other woman near. He was fine. He was the color of mocha and chocolate. He was God's wild child. She couldn't plan out her life with him because she didn't know what was around every corner; but she knew she could hold on tight when they rounded every corner. But she planned to hold on tight as they both discovered life. The thought made Lisa chuckle out loud, which turned Ken's head towards her.

Ken looked at her askance, and Lisa knew he must wonder at the softness of her gaze. He took it in for a bit but turned away. Lisa liked the new Ken that hesitated because he believed she and Banks were still involved.

"My mom taught me how to play poker. Did I ever tell you that?" he asked.

"No."

"She did. Of course, my dad hated it. *'Mbanu, Kenechuckwu, no son of mine will gamble,'* he'd say," Ken mimicked his dad's Igbo accent. "But my mom taught me behind his back. She said a man needed to know how to read faces and school his own. And poker would teach me that. My business savvy comes from her even though I was trash at poker. But one thing I remember her saying was that the ace in a deck was the highest card. Not only was the ace the highest card, it enhanced the power of any other high card. My mom would say, *'Kene, you never let your ace go.'*" Ken turned towards Lisa again as he continued. "I'm a high card…but you're the Ace, Lisa. I don't want to let you go. And trust me, I tried. I…I know I may not the best man for you – " was all Ken got out before Lisa kissed his surprised lips.

Ken looked like he was dreaming, his lips still apart after Lisa broke their kiss.

"You are. You are what I want, Ken. You are just perfect for me," Lisa said hurriedly and barely above a whisper.

"And Bankole?" was all Ken could manage.

"We are no longer together. I broke things off. A while ago, actually."

Ken knew Lisa could see the ecstatic, albeit quiet, happiness on his face at *that* news. Lisa got up to a kneeling position and drew Ken up from where they'd both been sitting to the same kneeling position.

"Ken, I forgive you. I forgive you," Lisa repeated. "But you cannot operate or own strip clubs…ever again."

"Already done," Ken interjected. He would add later that he'd made that decision, not for Lisa but because of his newfound faith in God. Pastor Chi says God is now his Father. And the strip club business didn't sit well with his Father.

"And you cannot have *any* kind of interaction with Ije when she leaves prison."

"Who? Never met her."

"Good. Keep it that way," Lisa said through a chuckle.

Ken simply stared at her. It has been a long journey up to this point, a journey with many uncomfortable and painful detours. There was the asthma, the faith divide, the fracas with Pastor Dare, the burned building, the shooting, his mom's death, *Bankole!* The long winding road led Ken to exactly where he was now: on his knees in front of Lisa.

But Ken would do this the right way, if there was to be hope of having any semblance of a normal relationship with his father-in-law. He would formally ask Pastor Dare for Lisa's hand in marriage...again. This time, he wouldn't *tell* the man that *he* planned to marry Lisa, whether Pastor Dare agreed or not. Ken would ask in humility. Hopefully, Pastor Chi would speak up for him. Hopefully, Pastor Dare would not call down fire.

For now, Ken simply said, "I am yours, Ace. *Forever.*"

EPILOGUE

It was dedication day. Pastor Dare and Pastor Chi were on their Sunday morning walk to BESEM with their grandson between them. Ken and Lisa had arrived at the vicarage, so they could all walk to church together. Emeka was home, too. Though he'd finally moved out into his own humble apartment, he visited every Sunday and walked with his family to church.

"Higher! Higher, Pop-pops!"

"Swiiinnng!" Pastor Dare and Pastor Chi exclaimed playfully as they walked to BESEM with their grandson between them on a bright Sunday morning. They were swinging the fifteen-month-old who had double the dose of the energy for his age. His twin sister was the quiet one, currently nestled in her father's arms. Pastor Dare and Pastor Chi walked with their grandson in the front; Ken and Lisa were behind them with their daughter.

Ken and Lisa had now been married for just over two years. Though they'd wanted to wait to have kids, the twins had arrived within the first year of marriage to Lisa's surprise; she'd thought she'd covered all her basis while they honeymooned in Zanzibar. When she told Ken she was pregnant with twins, Ken hadn't been surprised at all. He'd given her one of his mischievous smiles as he relayed the dream Pastor Chi had told him. Ken had become closer to Pastor Chi than Lisa was to her own mom.

BESEM was dedicating the House of Merciful Embrace – HOME. Out of the ashes of Adagio, HOME sprung up a campus of three big buildings and one smaller one. Two buildings provided separate housing for male and female residents. The third building was the heartbeat of the campus. It was an adult vocational center primarily dedicated to residents but also opened to the public. Skills taught in the vocational center ranged from technical skills like coding and repairs of electrical appliances, to fashion designing, hair dressing and barbing. The smaller building was a clinic that provided free preventative care to all and free obstetrics and gynecological care to low-income women. Lisa worked out of that building more than at her own clinic. Though HOME was going to be officially dedicated to God today, it had been open for use for a few months.

Pastor Dare nestled his Bible against his chest with his left hand and held his grandson's hand with his right. Just as BESEM came into sight, Pastor Dare's granddaughter decided to switch carriers as she stretched her hands towards her grandpa. Pastor Dare didn't want to let go of his grandson, but he still wanted to hold his granddaughter.

"Here, I'll hold your Bible," Ken offered,

"Very well. Thank you, Kene" Pastor Dare replied.

The pair were seeing eye-to-eye on more matters these days. As grandchildren usually do, the arrival of the twins greatly softened Pastor Dare's heart towards Ken. Pastor Dare now considered Ken his son...the adopted one. Ken was simply glad he had his own family. And he was content to be closer to Pastor Chi than Pastor Dare. As Ken took the Bible from Pastor Dare and passed his daughter to the older man, a knowing look passed between him and Pastor Chi. *This* was Pastor Chi's second dream.

"Ken, I need to see Mama Abiye today. Her son texted me yesterday evening."

"Okay. Bosco can drive us there."

"Ken, you don't have to come with me."

"I'm not going to let you drive on Lagos-Ibadan Expressway alone."

"I've been doing it for years, Ken."

"And you're still going to…just not alone," he responded with a smile as they entered the church where a thunderous celebration was already in full swing.

The road to BESEM, like the Lagos-Ibadan Expressway, had yielded more discoveries than neither Ken nor Pastor Dare could have anticipated. One thing was sure, there are many more discoveries on these roads. Such, after all, is the nature of life. As they travel on this road, may there be pitstops of grace and mercy. May love help them navigate the busy roads. And may they never go it alone.

The end.

AUTHOR'S NOTE

Thank you for reading the conclusion of Ken and Lisa's story, which very much started as Ken and Pastor Dare's story.

As I mentioned, the idea for the first part of this book, *By Force, By Tulas*, came to me a few years ago as I was driving. This book was different. I went through many rewrites because it wasn't immediately clear to me how Ken and Lisa's story should end. I like Ken but there were times I didn't think he and Lisa should end up together. Then again, I felt the same way about Lisa.

I finally concluded that what we believe is one thing; how we live, however, is what really matters. Ken and Lisa are similarly situated in their walk of faith; they are still discovering who they are in Christ. And so, it made sense that they should be on the journey together.

I should let you know that Alaro village is entirely made up, as I don't think any such small village exists on the outskirts of Lagos.

Of course, I wanted to feature God in the story as the One who holds time in His hands. He gives and He takes as He pleases. He is sovereign like that. And He is always merciful and gracious. Like the first story, I hope this story encourages you to start a walk with God through Jesus Christ. I hope you know to turn to Him in your darkest hour. He wants to hear from you.

Please share your comments with me at Bakisanya1@gmail.com. You can also scan the QR code below to follow my Facebook page – 31 Thoughts. I'd love to hear from you!

Sincerely,
B. Akisanya

ACKNOWLEDGMENTS

To my three children and husband, I am ever in awe that I get to do life with you. I remain overwhelmed with gratitude when I think of God blessing me with each of you. To my mom and siblings, thank you for your constant support in every venture. You are proof that God's grace and love were following me before I knew what to do with them.

A big thank you to my pastors and church community. Thank you for the nurturing environment and for sharing your wisdom. Thank you for your example!

To God through Jesus Christ, it all belongs to You. May You find some use for this story, and may it bring glory to Your Name.

ALSO BY B. AKISANYA

Levirate

By Force, By Tulas

Strength & Light for The Anxious Mind
(A 52-week journal)

Protocols of His Presence –
For the heart that yearns for God

Made in the USA
Monee, IL
10 June 2025

18881089R00121